INSTANT ATTRACTION

LAUREN BLAKELY

ALSO BY LAUREN BLAKELY

Big Rock Series

Big Rock

Mister O

Well Hung

Full Package

Joy Ride

Hard Wood

One Love Series

The Sexy One

The Only One

The Hot One

The Knocked Up Plan

Come As You Are

The Heartbreakers Series

Once Upon a Real Good Time

Once Upon a Sure Thing

Once Upon a Wild Fling

Sports Romance

Most Valuable Playboy

Most Likely to Score

Lucky In Love Series

Best Laid Plans

The Feel Good Factor

Nobody Does It Better

Unzipped

Always Satisfied Series

Satisfaction Guaranteed

Instant Gratification

Never Have I Ever

Overnight Service

Special Delivery

The Gift Series

The Engagement Gift

The Virgin Gift (coming soon)

The Exclusive Gift (coming soon)

Standalone

Stud Finder

The V Card

Wanderlust

Part-Time Lover

The Real Deal

Unbreak My Heart

The Break-Up Album

21 Stolen Kisses

Out of Bounds

Birthday Suit

The Dating Proposal

The Caught Up in Love Series

Caught Up In Us

Pretending He's Mine

Playing With Her Heart

Stars In Their Eyes Duet

My Charming Rival

My Sexy Rival

The No Regrets Series

The Thrill of It

The Start of Us

Every Second With You

The Seductive Nights Series

First Night (Julia and Clay, prequel novella)

Night After Night (Julia and Clay, book one)

After This Night (Julia and Clay, book two)

One More Night (Julia and Clay, book three)

A Wildly Seductive Night (Julia and Clay novella, book 3.5)

The Joy Delivered Duet

Nights With Him (A standalone novel about Michelle and

Jack)

Forbidden Nights (A standalone novel about Nate and Casey)

The Sinful Nights Series

Sweet Sinful Nights

Sinful Desire

Sinful Longing

Sinful Love

The Fighting Fire Series

Burn For Me (Smith and Jamie)

Melt for Him (Megan and Becker)

Consumed By You (Travis and Cara)

The Jewel Series

A two-book sexy contemporary romance series

The Sapphire Affair

The Sapphire Heist

ABOUT

Indulge in a standalone romance that tells the interwoven tale of three couples in New York City in a naughty modern fairy tale.

And in this once upon a time tale, you'll meet a circle of friends. There are friends who want to become lovers, colleagues who must resist an office romance, and fake dates that might turn into the real thing.

But all those stories start with *instant attraction*...

When hipster Gavin suddenly finds his best friend Savannah utterly irresistible...

When charming Enzo thoroughly falls for taken successful, sophisticated Valerie though he's contracted to work with her company...

When Jason meets his best friend's feisty and fun sister, Truly, for the first time...

Grab your popcorn and devour this ensemble romance of three interconnected couples whose lives intersect as they fall in love.

PROLOGUE

Once upon a time, in a land smack-dab in the center of everything worth mentioning, there lived a circle of friends.

They were friends who hooked up with friends, with roomies, with best friends' sisters, despite there being rules against such things. They hooked up with long-time crushes and with short-time acquaintances who became much more.

Some got together quickly, and some took years. Some needed a road trip out of the city to make them let go and go for it. Others needed one night.

And some need a little help from their friends. A little hint, a gentle nudge, and voilà!

Love at first bang.

What? This is a modern fairytale, and we like them a little dirtier—okay, *a lot* dirtier, full of flirty texts and sexy selfies, stolen moments, and dates that turn into sleepovers that turn into waking up in each other's arms with the promise of pancakes.

I've been lucky enough to live my love story— Spencer Holiday, the playboy who fell hard and fast for his best friend while pretending to be engaged to her. That's me. Now I'm setting the stage for my friends with sexy fairytales of their own.

Because everyone deserves a naughty love story.

1

GAVIN

Some things are undeniable from the get-go.

You dig a band the first time you hear them.

You prefer chocolate over vanilla.

And you will never, ever want to be set up with someone your mother claims is a perfect match.

My mother's been on a set-up-her-son bender since my status shifted to single a few months ago, so I naturally presume when she calls me at midday on a Wednesday that she's persisting with that plan of attack.

I'm at work, so I step out of the booth at the recording studio owned by the indie label I work for. One of our bands is cranking on some new tunes. Marge Simpson's face disappears from the screen as I swipe to answer the call.

What can I say? Mom reminds me of the cartoon character. She doesn't have blue hair, but she's totally the woman in charge. Hence, Marge.

"Hey, what's up, Marge?"

Also, her name is Marge, so she'll never know it's her nickname too. Yeah, I'm clever like that.

"Gavin, I have amazingly exciting news!" It comes out like a song.

I decide to toy with her since, well, that's always fun to do. "You're hosting a massive retirement party on a cruise ship that's going to take you across the Atlantic Ocean and all the way around the coast of Norway, where you'll finally meet that handsome Nordic man you've always been dreaming of?"

"How dare you say that? I'll be loyal to your father until the end."

"But someday, I know you're going to find that hot Viking guy. I've seen your book collection. The secret is out."

She tuts. "Your father *is* the hot Viking guy."

I run a hand over my chin. "True. He is where I get my strapping Nordic god looks from."

"And me. Don't forget I contributed half of your handsomeness."

"Yes, my charming Greek heritage," I say as I wander down the hall, running a hand through my dark hair.

"Which brings me to the point of this call."

I arch a brow. "You want to discuss my heritage? Ma, is this when you tell me I'm the love child of a secret tryst you had on the Love Boat?"

"Sweetheart, shh. It was on the HMS Shag at Sea."

I cringe. "One, I don't want to know you shagged

ever. Two, how did I not know you've seen *Austin Powers?*"

"Everyone's seen *Austin Powers*. Don't be silly." She takes a breath—the kind that signals she has big news to share. "In any case, back to your charm and my news. As you know, your sister is engaged, and I'm so excited that I'm throwing a party."

"Because she found somebody who wants to marry her? I know, it shocked me too," I say, teasing.

"Don't talk that way about Gretchen. She's very happy with Todd. And I've been thinking lately how wonderful it would be if you met someone who makes you as happy as Todd makes Gretchen. What do you think about that absolutely fantastic idea?"

My mom and her matchmaking. She's been relentless since I was in high school. She'd call me during college, suggesting different women in the dorms. After I graduated, she'd attempt it with ladies in the neighborhood. The fact that she set up my sister with her financial planner—*Mom's* financial planner—has only fueled her belief that she knows how to mix and match her kids.

"That's great that Gretchen is so happy," I say, attempting to steer the conversation.

"Isn't it?" Mom says, sighing happily. "And I just thought, love is in the air, so let's grab it, bottle it, and make it work for you."

She's not only driven by her past success—singular. She's also convinced I'm failing in life without a partner. Admittedly, I did wash a red sock with my whites a few weeks ago, but I don't think that's proof that it's time for me to settle down.

And fine, my fridge only has mustard and beer inside it, but this is New York. No one has anything but condiments and booze in their homes.

I'm not interested in locking down my options. And it's not because I'm a player. I'm not banging a new woman each weekend. I had a steady girlfriend for several months until she took off recently.

FOR ANOTHER GUY.

Suffice to say, I'm not that interested in being matched with anyone. I'm not interested in commitments that might go up in flames. And I definitely don't want to be blindsided ever again.

Best to be single for now.

I turn and pace the other way down the hall. "I don't know that I'm really ready for a bottle of love, Mom. But that would make a fun title for a song."

"Yes, tell one of your bands. Because love makes people happy. You think you're not ready, but *of course* it's time for you. Let me set you up. I'm so good at it. You know, I did used to be an HR manager."

"I know, Mom. I was literally raised by you."

"And being an HR manager means I have excellent people skills," she says, continuing to tout her setup abilities.

I stop outside the studio, gazing in through the glass at the engineer and my empty chair. I'm one of the managers here, and I need to get back in there and manage. "Your people skills are the best, Mom. But that doesn't mean I want to be set up." I need to be firm with her or she'll never let it go.

She huffs. "How long are you going to be on this dating sabbatical?"

"Mom, I appreciate your efforts, but I don't have a clock. I'm going to be on the sabbatical as long as I need to be on the sabbatical."

"I understand, but I think it's time for the sabbatical to end. And your sister's engagement party would be a wonderful opportunity to say goodbye to your dating diet. I think Christine from Gretchen's book club would be fantastic. She's well-read and loves music. She's perfect for you."

At first, I'm surprised she mentions Christine, but then I'm delighted because I can mess with my mom. "By loving music, I presume you mean the fact that she's an avid Taylor Swift fan. And hey, Taylor kills it, but that's the extent of Christine's musical knowledge and interest. Also, she *never* reads the book club books. She admitted that to me."

"Hmm. How unusual."

"No, it's quite usual. A lot of people fake it through book club. But don't you want to know how I know this?"

"How do you know those details about Christine?"

I stop in my tracks and drop the mic. "You set me up with her like three years ago. It didn't work out then."

"Ohhh." A self-deprecating chuckle comes next. "Well, isn't that proof I'm always thinking of my son?

But you're so insistent on saying no that it makes me wonder." She says it like a detective assembling clues. "Are you seeing someone and haven't told me yet?"

Oh.

Wow.

Holy shit.

She's offering me an out. And all I can think is —*take it*. Just fucking take it.

I don't think. I jump. Right off that cliff—a hundred feet high and straight into the water. And as I'm falling into the cool blue, I tell her, "As a matter of fact, I am seeing someone."

When I say goodbye to Marge, I need to figure out who the hell that's going to be.

2
———

GAVIN

Tonight, I'm having a beer with my best friend at our favorite bar in Williamsburg.

"Now all I have to do is find someone to bring along to the engagement party," I say as I thank the bartender for the IPA then take a drink.

"How about your receptionist? She's pretty fucking foxy," Eddie offers, lifting his glass and knocking back some of his drink.

I stare at him like he just suggested we shop for new bath towels. Eddie believes towels never age. "The receptionist at Glass Slipper is foxy?" I say. "She's like fifty years old."

Eddie narrows his eyes. "And you don't think fifty-year-old women are foxy? Don't be ageist, Gav. Just because you're twenty-nine doesn't mean a fifty-year-old woman can't be foxy."

I hold up my hand. "Okay, I am one hundred

percent not ageist, but I just had no idea you had a thing for her."

He shoves a hand through his floppy hair. "Dude. I have a thing for pretty much every woman."

I laugh as I knock back some beer. "Yeah, that's pretty much true."

Eddie is nondiscriminatory. It's pretty simple to be Eddie.

He stretches his arm across the back of the barstool. "Don't avoid the issue. We need to discuss the fact that you're an ageist. Do I need to take you to sensitivity training? I expected better of you, man."

I laugh. "Yes, please. Because it's so insensitive not to consider Sally Jo as dating material on account of the fact that she has three grown kids. Also, she's married."

He snaps his fingers, frowning. "Damn. All the good ones are taken." His expression lights up again. "Hey, how about that stripper? Angelina. Or Angelica. Or Angel. Why don't you take her to the party and pretend she's your date?"

I shoot him a look like he can't be serious. "That was you who dated the lady-cop stripper. Not me. Don't you remember your b-day?"

He drops his jaw. "Shit. You're right. I did date the stripper. And you know what? She was a sweetheart. A total doll."

"Also, her name was Lisa."

"Her real name was Lisa?"

"No, her stripper name was Lisa."

"Ah, you're right. Angel's the woman who walked my friend's ferret in Prospect Park. The stripper was Lisa. Sweet, leggy Lisa."

I roll my eyes, laughing as I down more of the beer. "You dated her because she was a sweetheart? Is that what you want me to believe?"

He sighs happily as a tune by The National floats through the neighborhood dive bar we frequent. "She was the kind of stripper you take home to Mom."

"I didn't know there were strippers you took home to Mom. Also, this song rocks."

"The National always rocks. But don't be talking music to distract me from your scathing words about women who work the pole." He narrows his eyes at me. "There are all kinds of strippers. I'm not ashamed of taking one home to my mother."

"Because your mom runs an escort service. Your mom was the one who taught us about sex." I laugh. "Like that wasn't totally fucking weird."

"It was a little weird. I'll give you that one, buddy. But she does quite well with her business. Also, she's totally cool, and she would have no issue with you dating a stripper."

"My mother, on the other hand, is not at all like that. Even though she likes to be all pals and buddy-buddy. So I can't take a stripper to my sister's party. Which is fine, because I don't actually want to."

Eddie sets his beer on the counter, signals for another, then mimes rolling up his sleeves. I don't think he owns a shirt with rollable sleeves; they're all of the T-shirt variety. "Okay, let's figure this out. Let's get a date for the Gav man after Denise dumped his ass."

I shoot him a stare. "Gee. Thanks for reminding me of that."

He claps my shoulder. "Hey, don't be ashamed of being dumped. All the good guys have been dumped. I've been dumped. You've been dumped. It's a rite of passage. I only mention the dumping because it's going to make it that much sweeter when you find the woman you're meant to be with."

Eddie is a strange mix of crass and, well, romantic. He does believe in true love. He believes it's coming for him, for me, for everyone.

The door to the bar opens, and in walks my coworker and good friend, Savannah Waters. Her hair cascades down her neck to her shoulders, and her trim figure catches my eye. But it always does. Empirically and all. She's a friend, but she's also a foxy friend. Eddie whips his head around and calls out to her, "Yo, Savannah. Come here." Eddie pats the stool next to him.

She joins us, her dark-blonde hair framing her face. "I'm meeting Sloane and Piper in a few minutes, but what can I do for you two troublemakers?"

"Who says we're making trouble?" I ask with an *I'm so innocent* smile.

She arches one eyebrow, and the look on her face is a little flirty. It's a good look on her. A look I like.

"Isn't that what you do?" she asks. "You cook and stir it up like a couple of chefs."

"We have a vat brewing in the back," Eddie says.

"Just add a little sriracha." She leans against the bar. "Some hot sauce and I'll have it like soup."

I hold up a hand. "I want this trouble soup, especially if it's extra spicy."

She gives me a droll look. "Always spicy. I *always* like it spicy. That's my mantra."

Mine too. Food, sex, you name it.

"Screw mild" is my answer, and she responds with a wiggle of her eyebrows.

Briefly I wonder if Savannah likes it spicy or sweet in the bedroom, but then I strip that thought from my mind. We're friends, and I'm not looking for anything more.

Eddie waves a hand, big and bold. "I got it!" He clamps the hand on Savannah's shoulder. "Ask her to be your date."

3

SAVANNAH

Look, I'm not going to lie. I've kind of, maybe, sort of had a thing for Gavin for a long time.

As in, since I started working at Glass Slipper Records a couple years ago, handling PR for a number of our top acts. It's not just a looks thing, because I'm not just a looks gal.

But he has those. Oh hell, does he have a fabulous face, great hair, and eyes that mesmerize me.

But looks fade.

What caught my eye and still ignites my brain is the way he holds the door for me and how we can endlessly obsess over music together, and the fact that he loves to try new food trucks at the farmers market near our office.

Plus, he remembers my coffee order. And I don't know why that's some magical thing that guys do, but it feels like it is. When a guy bothers to remember your coffee order and that you like your Thai food extra spicy, and thinks that you would love this cool new girl band that Glass Slipper signed (and he's right)—that's the someone you should be thinking of as boyfriend material.

Except . . .

There's one little issue.

He's had a girlfriend for a chunk of the time I've worked here, so we've been friends.

Just friends.

That's why I zipped up my crush and then motherfucking stomped on it. I stubbed it out so hard that I stopped thinking of him that way, and now he is only and absolutely a friend. A very good friend.

And he's the kind of friend I want to keep.

So it's with *only* a friendly curiosity that I latch on to Eddie's comment, meeting Gavin's blue-eyed gaze as I ask, "What do you need a date for?"

"Well, it's not *really* a date," he says quickly. I try not to let the cheetah speed of his response bother me. Who cares that he doesn't see me as date material? We are friends and that's fine by me.

"Ha! Yeah! Exactly. No real dates going on here," Eddie says, chuckling as if the idea of dating me is the height of comic relief.

Gavin gives his best friend a sharp stare.

"You're friends. You're one of the buds," Eddie explains, smacking me on the arm then administering a series of very friendly punches. Male punches. "That's why you're perfect for this. Our boy here needs a fake date because his mom is riding his ass about his single status."

"Ah, the plot thickens," I say in my best spooky voice. It's better than letting on that Eddie's comments bum me the hell out, since he obviously knows Gavin's true heart.

But then, why should I be bothered that they see me as one of the crew? Gavin and I are friends and have been for the last couple years. I'd ruthlessly squashed any wish for more, so there's no reason to be saddened that Gavin doesn't want more either.

"My mom is definitely on my case. I have to go to a party this weekend, and she wants to set me up with, like, a million women from the neighborhood. And I'm just not into my mom setting me up," he says with a casual shrug.

I drum my fingers on the bar, understanding his situation. "If I let my mother set me up, I would be dating the butcher."

"The butcher? Why?" Gavin asks.

"She works right next door to him, and she's convinced he's the perfect man for me."

"You don't even like meat," Gavin says, with an inquisitive lift of his eyebrow.

"Exactly!"

"So, again, why the butcher?"

I wave a hand airily. "Seems he's interested in getting married, and like most mothers, mine is obsessed with grandkids, so she figures if I take up with the butcher, I'll be popping out babies nine months later."

Eddie rubs his hands together. "The butcher is knocking up Savannah on their wedding night. Go, meat man!" He pats my stomach. "The butcher is going to put a baby meatball in the Sav-meister's belly."

I shoot him a glare. "Meat man? Meatball? Eddie, where do I even start dissecting everything that's wrong with that?"

Gavin raises a hand. "I feel like meat man is a good place to start."

Eddie shakes his head, heaving an indignant sigh. "The two of you are ballbusters. So what if Gav wants to date strippers and Sav wants to bang butchers?"

I snap my gaze to Gavin. "What? Strippers?"

Gavin slices a hand through the air. "He's just being . . . Eddie."

"And you two are being offensive to the noble industry of removing clothes for money," Eddie adds with a pout, overdoing the put-upon routine.

I hold my arms out wide. "Date strippers, date butchers, date go-go dancers, date girlfriends-for-hire. I'm not judgy."

Eddie points at me. "See? She's the perfect fake plus-one for you. She's totally chill."

"And we're back to the fake date for your mom's benefit." I scan the bar for Sloane and Piper, since we're meeting for a game of pool. Neither is here yet, though, so I stick with the guys. "What is it about moms that makes them want to set you up? And usually with the completely wrong type of person."

Gavin's blue eyes twinkle as if we're speaking the same language. "Right? Because we spend our whole lives trying to avoid being our parents or having the same taste as them. And then all they want to do is meddle in our love lives."

"So it's settled, then." Eddie claps Gavin on the back and squeezes my shoulder. "You guys will be fake dates."

Eddie raises a finger, signaling the bartender, and as he places an order, Gavin looks at me, vulnerability in his crystal blue eyes. "Do you mind though?"

My heart beats a little faster, and my pulse hammers a little harder, all from the way he looks at me. Like he cares about me. Like he wants to make sure I'm truly good with this. "No, I really don't mind. I mean, that's what friends are for, right?"

He drags his hand across his forehead like he's relieved. "Yeah. And you are an awesome friend, Savannah. I am so grateful. I'm just not ready to go to this event and have my mom arrange a plus-one."

"And you're probably not even ready to date again," I offer, and then I wonder why I'm saying that. Why am I pointing out that it's too soon? Oh right, I'm doing it because it's my armor. Buckle it on, tighten it up. I need the steel covering to protect myself, lest he realizes I once wanted more from him.

"I haven't really dated since Denise left," he says.

The mention of her name makes my jaw tick. I

hate that Denise hurt him. How could she not see what she had in front of her? Ingrate.

"I hear ya. You're not ready to get back out there," I say.

"Exactly. But I do need help. You don't mind?"

"I don't mind at all," I say, as the front door swings open and I spot a mane of blonde hair and a pair of big brown eyes. "Listen, Sloane's here, but we should come up with a plan. Backstory and all that."

"Let's make a date," he says, then corrects himself. "I mean, to plan our backstory."

We agree to meet before the party to spin our fairy tale, and I tell myself I don't care that it's all make-believe.

4

SAVANNAH

Sloane arches a brow as she pulls back the pool cue, giving me an "I can't believe you did that" lecture with just one look. I suspect I'm about to receive an earful too.

"So, let me get this straight," she says, eyeing the red ball as she lines up her shot. "The guy you're into asked you to go on a fake date."

I gulp, then put on my best confident face. "Yes. He did. But I'm not into him anymore."

"Right." She studies the table then meets my gaze. "And you said yes?"

"I said yes."

She nods like a professor employing the Socratic method. "And you thought this was a good idea?"

I lift my chin. "Sure. He needs help."

"And you don't think that's a recipe for disaster?"

"Why would it be a recipe for disaster?"

She shoots me another knowing look. That's the

thing about good friends. All of Sloane's looks are knowing because she pretty much knows everything about me.

I try to make light of my decision. It's going to be fine. I've been friends with Gavin for a while now, and it's all good. "I don't see why it would be a recipe for disaster," I say, leaning on my pool cue. "Besides, it wasn't even really him who asked, so it's not like it means anything."

Sloane pulls back the cue and lightly taps the white ball, sending the red one rolling across the green felt and into the corner pocket.

"Nice." Even though we're competing with each other, I can't help but admire such a beautiful shot.

Sloane and I are something of a pair of pool sharks. Since I was raised by parents who made pool balls, bocce balls, and croquet balls, I was encouraged in all leisure pursuits from a young age, ranging from music to crochet to pool.

"Thanks," she says and returns to the topic. "And this fake date—it wasn't even arranged by the guy you crush on, but by Eddie? Crazy, no-filter Eddie had the bright idea for Gavin to take you to his sister's engagement party?"

"Yes. It'll be fun," I say, all cheery and peppy. But I do think the party will be entertaining. "Gav and I have a great time together. We have fun when we grab lunch, and we had a blast playing badminton on the company team. He's a good, good friend."

Sloane smirks, nodding several times as she lines

up her next shot. "Oh, yeah. He's a *great* friend. A friend you harbor no feelings for or fantasies about."

I draw a deep breath. I'll convince her with my certitude. "If I was able to shut my feelings down the entire time he was involved with Denise, I can do it now. And the party *will* be fun."

"You don't think it'll be, how shall we say, *tempting?*" Her lips go all sexy pouty, making it clear exactly where she thinks the party will lead.

Scoffing, I shake my head. "It's just a party. Now, come on, keep going," I say, urging her to take another shot.

She works her way around the table, and when she misses the purple ball, it's my turn, and I angle myself toward the middle pocket.

But before I can start, she beckons me, her fingers waggling, and dresses her voice in a whisper. "Don't let him take advantage of you."

My brow knits. "What do you mean? How the hell is he going to take advantage of me?"

"Who's taking advantage of who?" The bold question comes from our friend Piper, who's just sauntered in looking fashionable and perfectly put together. Piper is vibrant and outgoing and hates to miss any juicy gossip. "Tell me everything."

"If you're going to arrive late, you're not going to get all the details," Sloane says, chiding her before she gives her a quick hug. I'm next—we're huggers and I love my girls, even when they gang up on me.

Sloane motions for Piper to come close and points

my way. "Gavin Hot Pants Clements just asked her to be a fake date at his sister's engagement party, and I don't want him to take advantage of her soft, gooey side."

Piper's brown eyes go wide, and she rubs her hands. "Ooh. I nominate myself to plan your wedding when this gets serious. On account of your soft, gooey side when it comes to him."

I roll my eyes once, and then again, just to reinforce how nonchalant I am about this. "It's not going to happen. We're just friends. I'm going with him as a friend. Don't you understand that I can actually just be friends with him without it turning into anything more? There is nothing soft and gooey going on. Also, gross."

Sloane smirks then holds up her fingers. She counts off on three of them. "Three times. You just said you're *just friends* three times."

"Because we are," I insist.

Piper winks at me. "Sure. We get it."

I wave the stick at the two of them, poking Piper's arm then Sloane's hip. "I swear the two of you read way too many romance novels. You think everything is going to turn into something." A poke in the thigh. "Sometimes things turn into nothing." A poke on the wrist. "In fact, most of the time they turn into nothing. Maybe try reading some nonfiction, and you would know that."

Sloane scoffs haughtily then turns to Piper. "Can you believe she is mocking our reading habits?"

Piper holds up a stop-sign hand, going all California girl. "*As if.* Don't even talk to me anymore. I love romance. You should too."

I set down the cue, sighing. "Romance is my jam. But I'm a realist. Look around." I gesture to the pool area and the bar beyond. "The world is a wild, crazy place. And only true, crazy romantics would actually believe that something like pretending to be his date —at his sister's engagement party, no less—would turn into anything more. That just doesn't happen."

Piper purses her lips. "I beg to differ. As a wedding planner, I see romance bloom in all sorts of ways every day."

"Right. But in regular ways. Online, at work, in the gym. Not in *this* way. Therefore, the fact that I've had a crush on the guy is a moot point. In fact, I'm going to get online later and go through my Match.com requests, because there is no way anything will happen with my *good friend Gavin.*"

Sloane cuts in. "Are you sure though?"

"One: I may not have mentioned this, but we're friends. Two: we're coworkers. Three: he's not ready for more. Four: let's focus on something useful, like how to make this fake date believable. Because, five, here's how stuff works in the real world: he meets some hot girl online who looks just like the other girl he dated, he rebounds with her, and I continue providing a shoulder to lean on. Meanwhile, I eventually get over my crush on him and move on with some other sexy, music-loving hipster. Or a lumberjack maybe. That's how it works."

Piper raises her hand. "That's how it works *sometimes*. But let's talk about the whole 'is someone ready' notion." She takes a beat, gathering herself to make her point. "Whether someone's *ready* is a pointless argument. Love doesn't come when anyone is ready. Love sneaks up and bites you on the ass at the most inconvenient times. I should know—look what happened to me. It's not like I was expecting anything with Zach," she says, going all soft at the mention of her guy.

I set a hand on her arm. "Maybe not. Point is, it didn't happen in any crazy way. You got together in a very natural way." I turn to Sloane to bolster my case. "And the same with you and Malone. You worked together, and then you got back together. Case closed."

Sloane hums doubtfully. "There was a little more to it than that. But be that as it may . . . let's go over some tips to help you get through this event."

I breathe a sigh of relief. "Yes. Please. All I want is to make this believable."

Sloane wiggles her brows. "So you *don't* want it to be obvious that you're in love with him?"

I glare death rays at her. "I hate you."

Piper gives a big smile. "You love us."

"I hate you with the fire of a thousand suns."

"No. You love us the same way."

"Obviously," I grumble.

Sloane raises one finger. "But you're not wrong. First tip: let on that you want to have sex and make babies with him."

"I don't!"

"Don't be too touchy-feely," she adds.

"I wasn't going to," I insist.

"But do be just touchy-feely enough," Sloane continues.

"A hand here, a brush there," Piper adds. "You never know."

I set down my pool cue and cover my ears. "Stop. Just stop!" I uncover them. "You two are no help. I'm going to reread today's post from The Modern Gentleman in New York. It's about asking a friend when you need help, which is the *only reason* why Gavin asked me to be his fake date."

Piper gives me a look that's full of surprise. "You read that?"

"It's a really good blog. You read it too?" I ask.

"Of course. My friend Jason writes it. It's good to know what men are thinking," she answers.

"And men think of friends when they need a plus-one." I exhale. "That's why Gavin and I are getting together before the party to come up with a backstory."

"Yeah. That doesn't sound like a romance novel at all," Piper mutters.

I tap the felt. "Let's play, so I can destroy you two."

Later that night, after I win, I reread The Modern Gentleman in New York column again.

It's the necessary reminder of who I am.

I'm his friend.

Nothing more.

From the Blog of The Modern Gentleman in New York

Let's face it. Guys don't like to ask for advice.

It's not in our nature. Hell, our bloody DNA is twined with chromosomes instructing us to never ask for help when it comes to directions, driving, and, naturally, dating.

Just picture the standard-issue dad back in the day, map to his holiday destination folded in a haphazard mess across the steering wheel, ignoring the anguished pleas from the rest of the car that he stop and ask for directions.

Map mishaps are rare now thanks to GPS, one of the greatest inventions since beer and rock and roll, the internet being sufficiently cool to circumvent a man's stubborn nature and allow him to ask for help.

And help is what I aim to give you today. The question of the day hails from Rhett, an intrepid reader who has a question about dating etiquette. Or rather, dating demands.

Rhett says: "I've been invited to a work event next weekend. A gala, if you will, and my boss told me I should bring a date. Do I actually need to bring one, and if so, do I just go to Tinder or Match to find one?"

Ah, the plus-one dilemma. We modern gentlemen face

*this all the time. But let me share my best advice with you.
Are you ready? Come closer. A little closer. Closer still.*

DO NOT FIND YOUR DATE ON TINDER.

There. I said it. I feel better.

Wait. There's more.

DO NOT FIND YOUR DATE ONLINE.

*Look, unless you're paying for some sort of service—and
hey, there's nothing wrong with platonic escort services—I'd
recommend a simple, straightforward solution: ask a friend.*

INTERLUDE

Spencer

Things might get a little interesting and perhaps a little complicated for Gavin and Savannah.

They're good friends, and she's going to pretend to be dating him while pretending she hasn't wanted to do that for ages. After all, Savannah doesn't even believe in *that* kind of romance. As for Gavin . . . I have a hunch he'll soon be looking at her with new eyes.

Did I say "a little complicated?" I should revise that. I bet everything is about to get a lot more complicated for those two.

Because that whole "ask a friend" thing . . . when has that ever been simple?

I asked a friend to be my fake date, and look how that wound up—as a big old serving of happily ever after.

But before getting back to these two, let's see what's cooking for that guy who just gave the advice on asking a friend.

For that we go back in time a little more than a few years ago to the night when a certain woman meets a certain man for the first time.

My wife's best friend, Truly, is going about her business, mixing drinks at a bar in Chelsea in the heart of Manhattan, when lo and behold, a man walks in who catches her eye.

Spoiler: Truly has no idea this guy is friends with her brother.

That's gonna be such a bummer.

5

TRULY

It's a question I've heard many times at my establishment, and it starts with *Would you rather . . . ?*

Bartenders hear the same things over and over. I could make a list, starting with the lines the guys use to hit on the girls. Because the bar pickup line is alive and well.

We might be living in a postmodern world of online dating, but there's still plenty of romance—and hookups—that ignite in person.

I'm betting on the latter happening right in front of me, based on the persistence of a goatee-sporting guy at the bar. He clears his throat and says to the brunette next to him, "Would you rather walk on hot coals or step on a sea urchin?"

The woman with the slim gold chain around her neck laughs. "I'd have to say walk on hot coals, because I'm actually pretty fast."

Uh-oh. That's only going to intrigue him more.

His dark eyes glint. "Fast, you say?"

She giggles. "Not like that. But give me another."

He rubs his palms together. "I'd love to give you more. Would you rather have fur or scales?"

Scales. Pick the scales, I want to say. Because this guy is going to take you home and never call you again. Scales make you seem tougher.

Alas, she picks fur and gets the same response he gave when he used the line last night on a different woman: "I bet yours would be so soft."

Gag.

He continues, sliding closer to his prey as I mix his mojito.

"Would you rather eat the same meal every day or never use Instagram again?"

She shudders. "Eat the same meal. Hello, I love Instagram."

I hand him his drink. "Here you go."

"Thanks so much," he says, then takes a sip and begins another round.

I'm so tempted to cut in and say, *Would you rather have a dragon or be a dragon?* Because that was another question he asked last night.

But it's not my job to intervene. Not unless things go too far. And nobody likes a bartender who acts as a policewoman.

"Would you rather wear roller blades on one foot or be stuck walking behind someone who goes too slow?" he asks, and I'm grateful when a new pack of customers streams in and I tend to them.

* * *

A little later, Charlotte arrives at Gin Joint, pulling up a stool at the bar and flashing her trademark smile. "Tell me everything. What kind of night has it been? What are you up to? How about customers?"

"We had a rather intense game of Would You Rather going on earlier," I say, then update her on what went down. "And then he left with her a few minutes ago. So I guess that means no cake for me."

She arches a brow in question. "How does the lack of cake follow a sleazy round of Would You Rather?"

My eyes go wide. "Didn't I tell you about the woman from a few months ago? The one who sent me chocolate the day after she was here? Then tulips, then daisies," I say, reminding my best friend of my new biggest fan.

"Yes! The redhead from the publishing house who met a hot suit at your bar," Charlotte says.

I nearly bounce. "They're getting married now, so she sent me a cake this afternoon as a thank you."

"Whoa. Are you trying to tell me you have cake you're not sharing with me?"

I tip my forehead to the back of the bar, where the cake is waiting for me. "It's really good cake too. Soft and moist and just the right amount of sweetness. Want a slice?"

"Grrr. I do. Except I already had a ginormous bag of gummi bears today, so I have to pass. But I'm also super jealous of your gifts."

"Who knew there were such perks to bar owner-ship? Normally it's just guys with the same lame 'would you rather' pickup routine."

Charlotte groans. "Ugh. They need new lines."

"They do. But this couple just had a normal conversation, made some jokes, and hit it off while I served them drinks. Just think of all the matches that might go down in my place that I can't miss."

"Maybe you'll meet someone tonight too," she says playfully.

I scoff at the ridiculousness of that notion. I'm not looking, not interested, and not planning on that happening. "Please. I'm not going to meet some guy at my bar. I'm working. And eating cake later." I wipe down the counter, switching subjects. "So how was softball? How did your man do?" I ask as I pour her an iced tea with a sprig of mint and a splash of grena-dine, her usual.

"Hubby's team won. I'm a good luck charm. Oh, did you hear that there's this new guy playing first?"

"Nope. The roster update didn't make it to me yet." Though I usually hear the details from my twin brother, Malone, who plays on the same team as Charlotte's husband, Spencer.

"Evidently—not that I notice that kind of thing because I'm very happily married—the new guy is kind of handsome . . ." She leaves that like a trail of gumdrops for me to follow.

I lift a brow. "And you're telling me this because?"

"Don't you have a catalog of handsome men?"

"Oh, yes, of course. It's incredibly long. I catalog all the handsome men in New York City. Then I look at it late at night while I'm eating bonbons."

She sticks out her tongue. "That was my way of saying *come to a game.*"

I tap my temple. "Ah, my Charlotte translator was off slightly. Now I get it. Unfortunately, I'm always here when the games are going on. But maybe I'll meet this guy another time," I say as I hand her the drink.

She takes a sip. "I bet you will. I think he's friends with your brother."

* * *

After Charlotte joins some friends and my mind returns to cake and happy couples, a tall, dark, and handsome man strolls into my bar.

Lots of tall, dark, and handsome men stroll into my bar. After all, this is Manhattan, and we grow that variety on trees.

But still, the fruit of this particular tree catches my eye. A faint dusting of stubble lines his square jaw, and his cheekbones are the floor model for the Strong and Carved line. Plus, he's wearing a tux, bow tie unknotted and the jacket slung over his arm. There's just something about a well-dressed man—he looks better than a sinful cake tastes.

He heads straight for my corner of the sleek silver bar, flashes a grin that contains the right amount of lopsided yumminess, and says, "Will I get in trouble if I don't order gin?"

And he speaks British. Cheers to me.

"Of course you'll get in trouble."

He smiles brightly. "But I'm in the mood for whiskey. Damn the consequences."

I smile and shake a finger. "You come into a gin joint and order whiskey? You're flirting with danger."

"Oh, is this going to be a bartender arrest? I've never been read my rights and tossed in the pokey, but I've always wondered what it would be like."

"Then I'm going to get out my handcuffs and chain you up."

He edges closer, parking his chin in his hand, his amber eyes sparkling. "That is a rather serious punitive action."

I set my hands on my hips. "I'm all about strict bar law enforcement," I say, and for the briefest of moments, I wonder if Charlotte was onto something. Maybe someday I will meet someone at my bar. Maybe someday is tonight.

"Then I suppose I should nix the whiskey and order something with gin?"

I smile my best sexy grin. "Don't you know? Everything tastes better with gin."

His eyes seem to roam over me, his gaze traveling down my face, landing on my lips. It should bother me that he's looking at me in this hungry, appraising way, but it doesn't. Would I rather he look at me hungrily or clinically?

Hungrily.

His lips hook into a grin, and my stomach flips. "I'm convinced. I want the gin drink *you* recommend. Have at it."

I take my turn surveying him up and down. "You look like you're in a fun sort of mood."

"I'm always in a fun sort of mood. Fun is my middle name."

"Is it short for something else?" I ask, playing along.

"Originally it was Funinsky."

"I see why you had to shorten it. Seems like it would be complicated to spell."

"Terribly difficult. Almost as hard as Extremely Amusing and Entertaining at All Hours of the Day." He taps his chest. "But that's my *other* middle name."

My eyebrows shoot up. "Wow. You really come with a lot of promises."

"I always make good on them."

"You are an entertaining and extremely amusing man," I say, shaking my head approvingly as I pour him the whiskey I suspect he truly wants. I slide him a glass. "Our best whiskey, since it'll suit your fun mood."

He lifts the glass. "Why, thank you." He takes a drink and licks his lips briefly, then sets it down and scans the surroundings. "And this is quite a lovely bar."

"As bar mistress, I thank you very much."

His eyes dance with mischief. "I suppose if one is going to be a mistress, that's the type one ought to be."

"Exactly. The only other kind I'd want to be would be a mistress of fun. Or cake."

"Cake," he says, dragging out the word like it's something decadent.

"Yes, *cake*," I say the same way. "It's on my mind, since someone sent me a delicious cake today."

He wiggles his fingers. "Don't hold back, woman. Give me a slice."

"It's not on the menu. I can't serve it to you. I'd be violating all the bartender laws."

"Ah, we'd have to cuff *you*, then."

"I suppose you would." I send a thank you to the gods of bar flow that we're slow for these few minutes on a Friday night. Someone is looking out for me, giving me this delightful chance to flirt with the most handsome and entertaining man I've met in ages.

"Tempting me with all this talk of cuffs and contraband—you're making me want this cake even more."

I motion for him to come closer, lowering the volume. "Later, I'll slip you a slice."

He groans, and it's ridiculously sexy. It's a needy, turned-on sound, and it makes my skin sizzle.

The trouble is my window closes. The gods of bar flow send a pack of customers in, and I need to take care of them. I excuse myself to mix and make drinks, and the whole time I'm thinking he's adorable and funny and clever and witty, and that we have an instant connection I'd like to return to.

But when I'm free, the sexy British man is gone.

My brother is here instead, heading straight for me. He says hello then glances around, his brow furrowing. "Have you seen my friend Jason?"

"Maybe, give me some more details on this person I've never met."

Malone laughs. "Ugly. Horrific British accent. Incredibly quiet and shy, never has a thing to say."

Kill. Me. Now. All the flirty, dirty butterflies in me do a facepalm. "That guy is your friend?"

He shoots me a curious look. "Yes. Why? Is that hard to believe?"

I plaster on a smile, cursing my luck. "It's not hard to believe. Not at all."

My shoulders sag a bit, and my libido shakes an angry fist at me.

No matter, I tell myself. I'm not about to go after one of my brother's friends. We've been down this road before and landed in a whole slew of trouble. It's simply not a road I'll travel again.

I draw a deep breath and tell myself that Jason must go into the friend zone. "We chatted here earlier, and he seemed like a lot of fun." That's an understatement.

My brother smiles. "Glad to hear that. I think you'll find him to be a good friend."

That's when the tall, dark, and handsome Brit returns to the bar, saying he had to step out to talk to a client, then he says to Malone, "And have you met the lovely bartender?"

My brother cracks up. "Yes. I've known her since birth."

Jason's jaw drops. To the freaking floor. He snaps his gaze to me. "You're his sister?"

"Not just any sister. I'm his twin."

Malone smacks his arm. "I told you we were going to my sister's bar."

Jason blinks like he's still processing this news. "Right, but I thought she was the bartender, not your sister."

Malone points to me. "Jason, meet my sister, Truly."

The man I felt an instant attraction to extends his hand, adopting a most professional expression. "Charmed."

"As am I."

It's true, and yet there's nothing to be done.

Would I rather pursue something with this tall, dark, and handsome man, or risk my relationship with my brother?

There is only one answer.

Jason and I must become friends.

6

JASON

"Punk rope? What on earth is punk rope?"

Truly laughs and gives me a look like I should know what this bizarre thing is she just suggested.

"What? Don't they have punk rope in London?"

"Is that your way of trying to say we don't have the latest trends in exercise across the pond?"

"I'm sure you do all sorts of crazy things. Like soccer and soccer and more soccer, and more soccer on top of that."

"Woman, how many times do I have to tell you it's called football?"

"How many times do I have to tell you I will never call soccer *football*?" She sets a glass down for me with such panache, it's a declaration.

I shudder. "Fine, have it your way. Your improper American way," I say, taking the glass and having a drink.

I had another wedding tonight, and it went off

without a hitch, so I'm here at Gin Joint to unwind. One more successful best-man-for-hire gig under my belt. "In any case, lest you think we're lacking in bizarre forms of exercise, I will have you know that we recently reinstated strolling classes."

"Soon, your homeland will work up to sauntering classes," she says with a sexy little lift of her eyebrows. Because everything she does is sexy.

"Of course, but it takes time for trends to reach there. As for punk rope, I'm not sure we'll ever see that in London."

"Good thing you're not in London, then," she says, wiggling her eyebrows, then pleading. "Come with me. You're my comrade in exercise. We're fitness warriors."

That's true. In the few months since I've met her, we've discovered we're both addicted to exercise, but we haven't worked out together yet.

"But what is punk rope? It sounds like we'd be in a mosh pit with a bunch of twine."

She grabs a glass of water from behind the bar and downs some. "It's like jump rope meets recess with cool music. Think of it as a PE class for adults set to rock and roll." She flutters her lashes. "Come along. Pretty please."

I give her a curious stare. "Why on earth are you asking me?"

She pouts. "You don't want to go with me?"

I need to think long and hard on my answer. I do enjoy Truly's company. An incredible amount. More than I probably should enjoy the company of my good friend's sister, since that's what Malone has quickly become.

And I do want to do all of these things with her. But I also know that it's a risk. The more time I spend with her, the more time I *want* to spend with her.

Then again, I've been tops at resisting anything remotely resembling a relationship ever since a particular woman back in London—ahem, Claire— saw fit to break my heart in half and then stomp on it with steel-toed combat boots, so it's not like anything with Truly is going to go further. I won't let it.

So I say, "Take me to your punk rope class, please."

She squeals in delight, and it's a sound I rather enjoy.

I'm sure I'd enjoy other high-pitched noises from her, but this will do. It'll do just fine.

* * *

The next day, I'm sweating buckets. My muscles scream. My brain struggles to keep up with a jump rope routine so complex it would take a degree in double Dutch to master. But at the same time, it's ridiculously fun.

When we're done, Truly and I are both laughing and sweating as she asks, "Do you want to grab a drink?"

"Do you actually drink at ten in the morning on a Sunday?"

She laughs, nudging my elbow. "I don't mean that kind of drink. A proper après exercise drink."

I shoot her the side-eye as we leave the YMCA and head into the Manhattan summer morning. "You can't possibly be suggesting we lose the benefits of that class by having a chocolate smoothie? Next thing I know, you'll be wanting to add peanut butter to it. And then what's the point? Woman, I do have to maintain my figure. As the premier best man for hire in all of Manhattan, I must keep up appearances."

She pats my belly. "It's flat. Flat as a board. And I would never ask you to put anything bad in that perfect body." My skin sizzles for a second at the way her eyes seem to roam over me.

Wait.

That heat lasts more than a few seconds because I do like her hand on my body.

"Please feel free to enjoy the washboard," I say.

She pokes her fingers across my abs and whistles. "Hot damn, Jason Reynolds. You do indeed have a six-pack."

"And you can inspect it anytime. Also, consider this my yes."

"Yes to what?" she asks curiously as we reach the crosswalk and wait for the light to turn.

"Yes to any fitness class you ever want to take, so long as it involves your hands on my belly."

"Well, it *was* fun to touch."

"And this is why I say no to smoothies. Cuppa?"

She adopts a posh British accent. "Why, yes. That

would be ever so lovely. And that's what I meant by après exercise drink, you weirdo."

"You're the weird one," I fire back.

We pop into a café around the corner, where she grabs a coffee and I order an English breakfast tea.

We chat about growing up in New York versus London, the relative merits of movie theaters versus streaming, and then the most unusual lines we've overheard—at bars for her and at weddings for me. When we're done, it occurs to me that I have a new friend, and I quite like this development.

But I also fully intend to keep her in the friend zone.

I can do that. I absolutely can.

Because I must.

INTERLUDE

Spencer

Ah, the good old friend zone.

So many of us wind up there. Some for a few days, some for years.

It's not necessarily a bad place to be.

There's something to be said about friendship as the basis for, y'know, *more*. In fact, friendship can be the perfect foundation for a whole lotta something more.

That's what I have with my wife—friendship and everything else.

So, hey, good luck, Jason and Truly, hanging out in that zone. The only questions now, I suppose, are how long they'll last there and whether anything can knock them out of it.

But for now, let's check in on some friends who face an entirely *different* set of complications: the dilemma of a filthy-rich woman and a man poised to become the next big thing.

Isn't there something fantastic about female billionaires? You don't hear their stories that often. But they can be pretty awesome—especially when they're strong, driven, and self-made.

And if she falls for the man she has to strike a business deal with, she could lose everything she's built. That would be quite a conundrum.

The course of love never did run smooth in Manhattan, but to get there, we'll have to detour to Las Vegas first.

7

ENZO

Growing up on the outskirts of Madrid with barely a shack covering my head and only ragged hand-me-downs to wear, my goals were simple: Make it out of the slums. Get an education. And when I'd made it, maybe find someone to share the good things in life.

At the time, I pictured running water, books, and three square meals a day. Never did I imagine art, culture, and all-expenses-paid trips all over the world. Nor did I dream I'd be in Las Vegas, a place as far away from our shack in Spain as the moon from Earth.

I had flown in for a book show. The romance writer Kat Riley asked me to attend a signing and sit at her table. So I find myself in a hotel ballroom, signing a woman's shirt.

The woman squeals. "Oh my God, I have every single book cover you've been on."

I smile as I write my name across the back of her

blouse—Enzo De la Rosa. "That makes me so happy to hear. And your shirt looks fantastic."

She turns around, giggling and trying to pat the back of the shirt. That proves challenging, so she brings her hands to her face and gasps. Then she lowers them, her brown eyes dancing with happiness. "You have no idea. You're my absolute favorite model. I buy every book you're on. All the Kat Riley books and all the others. The alien books. The cowboy books. The billionaire books."

"That is terrific. I hope you love them. That is great for the authors too." I beam—because I've done it. I've made it out. I'm supporting my family back home with my book covers, cobbling together a living from modeling.

The woman blows me a kiss, and I shoot a smile to Kat, who gives me a thumbs-up. "You're doing great," she says when the fan moves on. "I knew it would be smart to bring you."

Before I can sit, a redhead rushes to our table, gives a quick hello to Kat, then bestows her attention on me, shaking her hands out and taking a deep, shuddery breath. "I can't believe I'm actually meeting my idol."

"It's a pleasure to meet you," I say. Honestly, I feel a little bad because they do all seem to be here to see me. But I'm glad they're at least getting Kat's signature too.

"I've loved you since the alien books."

"As a young boy, I aspired to be an alien," I say, flashing a grin.

She gasps. "Gah! You're so funny. I loved it when your whole body was in blue for *Caught Up with the Alien Billionaire*. Please, God, let the sequel be *Swept Away with the Alien Billionaire's Secret Baby*."

"That was a fun shoot. I did enjoy that one."

She nibbles on the corner of her lips then takes another deep breath. "Do you think I could ever sign up to work on one of your shoots? If you ever need somebody to put blue paint on you, I'd be willing to do it."

Kat clears her throat. "I'll post a sign-up list for that ASAP." She stands, cups her mouth, and says to the line, "Who wants to put blue paint on Enzo De la Rosa? Show of hands?"

The crowd goes wild.

"Can you please do a blue alien again?"

"Please, please, please!"

"Invite all of us to come to your shoot."

"I'll pay if you let me put blue paint on Enzo!"

I blush, flashing a smile. "Ladies, ladies. You can all put blue paint on me."

* * *

A little later, a woman with red glasses and blonde streaks in her dark hair stands in front of me.

She extends a hand. "Gigi Williams. I'm an agent. Blue aliens are all well and good, but I can get you on billboards in Times Square. I can put you in TV commercials. I can get you in magazine spreads. There won't be a place where someone beautiful can be seen that you won't be."

I chuckle lightly. How many times have I heard that promise? How many times has it not been true? I won't let myself believe it. "Thank you very much, Gigi. But I've heard that before."

Her expression speaks only of confidence. "I completely understand, but I'm going to prove myself to you. I'll get you a gig in twenty-four hours."

I shrug happily. "Sure. If you do, I'm yours."

We exchange numbers, and I thank her for her enthusiasm, though I suspect it will amount to another round of blue alien covers, and that's fine by me. I've graced the front of fifty romance novels, and if I can keep working in this world and become the next Fabio, I will be a most happy man.

When the show ends, I help Kat pack up her sign and her swag.

"You're going to hit it big," she says. "You know that, right? Just remember me when you're on a bill-board in Times Square."

"Of course. But I don't expect to be there anytime soon."

I don't lack confidence. But neither am I so naïve that I believe that the world operates according to what's fair. Just because you're good at something doesn't mean you will make millions from it. There are many talented people, many beautiful people, many smart people who never make it big.

It's all about the right opportunity at the right time.

* * *

But this time is right, and the opportunity comes the next day when Gigi calls before I have to fly back to Spain.

"I booked you on a shoot for a T-shirt brand," she says.

My eyes widen. "Already?"

"I'm a woman of my word. Can you stay in the United States for a week?"

"I don't have any place to sleep."

"No worries. They will put you in a hotel in New York and I will send you out on other jobs."

That night as I fly to New York, I say a private thanks to the passionate book fans who love blue aliens and billionaires.

And over the next few years, I fly in and out of New York more times than I can count. I fly to Paris too, and Milan. Los Angeles as well.

It doesn't happen in the blink of an eye. But it *does* happen. My career takes off, and neither Gigi nor Kat were wrong.

I'm on billboards in Times Square and in ads for cologne and eyeglasses, for leather shoes and high-end department stores, for the highest of high-fashion brands, and for cars too. Those are my favorite, modeling with the sleek, sexy automobiles.

The new job gives me my heart's desire: the chance to buy a new home for my mother and my sister. To help my family have the life they've longed for.

To buy a work of art now and then.

Every time I do, I also purchase another book from Kat Riley as a thank you to the blue alien billionaire opportunity that changed my life.

One day after a shoot in Manhattan, I step into a gallery on the hunt for a new work of art, and I stop in my tracks.

I'm struck by the most beautiful piece of art I've ever seen.

And I must know her name.

8

VALERIE

I press the speaker button on my desk phone, calling my assistant. "Hello, Sadie. Please be sure to have that report on my desk by three p.m., and do get yourself some lunch today and charge it to me. I can't have you running around lunchless again. And no DoorDash. Please, for the love of Louboutin, *take a lunch break*."

"Of course, Ms. Wu. I'll have the report ready on time. And I'll DoorDash a chicken salad."

"You'll do no such thing. You'll leave and eat lunch out of the office, and I'll take care of it. You just enjoy yourself."

She takes a beat, then says, "If you insist. But then I'll have the report done by two-thirty."

I laugh. "That's what I love about you. Always exceeding expectations."

"Why would anybody want to do anything but exceed expectations for you? Also, thanks in advance for lunch."

"You're welcome. You need to eat."

I hang up, scrolling through the list of meetings I need to attend this afternoon.

I've learned that in business it's easy to be fearsome, but it's much harder to be kind. Yet you can succeed if you treat people well. And that's what I endeavor to do when my assistant delivers the report to me at two-thirty, right on time.

But punctuality isn't everything.

There is attention to detail, strategy, and insight. And as I peruse her report, I see that Sadie has given me that.

I meet her young gaze, her blue eyes framed by long lashes. "Sadie, this is fantastic. And in fact, you should leave at six instead of staying until eight to impress me," I say with a wink, so she knows I'm onto her.

"I don't think it'll impress you if I leave at six."

I grab my purse. "It will. Enjoy your life, or your whole life will be work. Now, I have a quick appointment with a business partner, but I don't want you to stay all night."

"I promise I won't. But I did have an idea for you," she says, her tone cheery, a good sign I'll like what she says.

"Oh, what's that? I do relish good ideas."

"Did you know there's a showing of David Harper's work at the Francesca Zurman gallery in Soho?" The glint in her eyes matches that chipper tone.

I gasp. "No! No. You can't be serious. How did I not know? How did *you* know?"

She shrugs playfully. "It's my job to find things that delight you. I snagged you a ticket."

"I adore you the most, and I command you to leave now and enjoy this city," I say, then I zip down from the top floor of the skyscraper that serves as my media empire's kingdom and head for the car waiting to whisk me across town to the meeting. Once that's done, I return to my office on wheels and make calls to our offices in Singapore, Auckland, Rio de Janeiro, and right here in Manhattan, where I check in with one of my colleagues on a new ad campaign we're spearheading, centered around the company's worldwide position in the media industry.

"Yes, and we just hired that new supermodel that's all the rage. He's like Gisele Bündchen but, you know, a guy," she tells me.

"Gisele pretty much is the template for successful models. And what is his name?"

"Enzo De la Rosa."

But I don't have time to google him. My car has arrived at the art gallery where I'm on the hunt for a new David Harper painting that would look fabulous in my living room here. Or maybe it would be better in my London home?

And as I'm looking over the pieces with a critical eye, a voice drifts to my ears.

A man's voice.

A man with a delicious Spanish accent.

"Ah, yes. That one looks incredible."

When I turn around, I see a face that was carved by angels.

9

VALERIE

It would be a cliché to say that our eyes lock.

So I won't say that. I will say that my eyes roam shamelessly up and down his body.

They wander all over his six-foot-something frame, his one-in-a-trillion face, and then meet deep brown eyes that seem to convey a thousand possible emotions.

But I've never been the type of woman who's attracted to a man solely for his looks. It's far too easy to find a good-looking vapid man, a good-looking cruel man, or a good-looking dim-witted one. Looks have never been enough.

I require a challenge.

Even though he's quite possibly the most handsome creature the universe ever crafted, I have no expectation that there will be a spark.

I head over to the painting that's caught his attention and study it closely. "I've always found his use of brushstrokes quite enigmatic, but at the same time, they reveal bizarre hidden truths about humanity."

The man whips his gaze to me, his eyes wide and brimming with curiosity. "Yes! It is as if he understands everything about our nature that we are struggling to hold on to and puts it somehow into his art."

A shiver runs down my spine. Another art lover. One who doesn't seem vapid at all.

I return my focus to the gorgeous tapestry of color in front of me. "You can see his depth of understanding in the way he constructs the figures and the way he tells the story. It makes this entire canvas come alive with meaning."

The man shakes his head in admiration, gazing at the art. "Sometimes I feel as if a piece of art can see inside my soul and elicit all the things I wonder about at the end of the day." He laughs, a self-deprecating sound. "Who am I kidding? I don't think about this only at the end of the day. I think about it *all day long*. If I didn't have art to stare at, my brain would be overrun with philosophical questions."

I chuckle. "I know what you mean. Art calms me too."

"The only thing I love more than trying to understand the meaning of art is acquiring it." He laughs in a sort of knowing way.

I toss him a curious stare. "Is that your dirty little secret? That you're turned on by art acquisition?"

His voice rumbles. "Turned on barely begins to cover it. It is one of my great passions. I absolutely love the chase. I love being able to track down a fantastic piece of art and win it before others do."

And that shiver that ran across my body? It turns into a full-blown tremble. Because this man is speaking my language.

I extend a hand. "I'm Valerie Wu. Pleased to meet you."

He flashes a smile that makes my stomach flip and my knees weaken. "Valerie, I am Enzo De la Rosa. What an absolute delight to meet you."

The new face for my company's campaign.

I cannot, not for a second, consider pursuing something with this man. Not if he is connected to my business.

Just. My. Luck.

I'll tuck all these naughty thoughts and delicious meanderings away in the lingerie drawer in my mind and then shut it tight, with nary a sexy silk strap peeking out.

Then he takes my hand and presses his lips atop my knuckles.

News flash: it is indeed possible to be turned on by a kiss on the hand.

Wickedly turned on.

Images now race through my brain—visions of the things I want him to do to me.

As a woman who spends days and nights striking

deals, managing and moving billions of dollars around, making decisions that affect hundreds of thousands of employees, there's little I love more in bed than letting go of all of that.

And the way Enzo looks at me with eyes that darken, with a manly, romantic confidence I haven't encountered in my forty-eight years, I know he could be exactly what I need.

But he's precisely what I can't let myself have.

He's a business partner.

I'm the CEO of a worldwide media company.

I simply can't tango with someone in my employ.

So even as we make more small talk about art and the flames spark through me, I deny them and deny myself.

"And now I must go. I understand you're the face of our new campaign. I'm so thrilled we're doing business together."

But he doesn't relinquish my hand. Instead, he holds it tighter, saying, "And perhaps someday soon it will be more than business."

On that lingering note of possibility, I turn and I walk out of the danger zone.

* * *

The next day, I bounce back and forth on my toes, wearing black shorts, a white sports bra, and my racquetball goggles. The blue ball whizzes at me at Mach speed. I slam it hard into the wall, and it zooms back quickly. Kingsley slams it right back at me. But I can't let her win. I need to channel this frustration.

Especially since I was up late last night thinking of that handsome young man.

Thinking vastly inappropriate thoughts.

Thoughts I must squash.

Like this ball.

I lunge for it, determined to win the match against my good friend. She's a fierce competitor though. One of the fiercest, and we have been playing racquetball against each other for years in our female CEO league.

With intense determination, I slam the ball one more time and win the game.

She curses. "You are evil, and I hate you."

"I accept your hatred. And I'm thrilled that's how you feel."

She laughs and grabs her water bottle, downing a gulp. I do the same, take a deep breath, then set down my racket as I adjust my sneakers. "Can we have a quick advice session?"

"Of course. I'm always up for advice." She places her bottle in her bag. "Fly in the ointment in a new business deal? How to handle a difficult employee? Which new markets to pursue next?"

"I wish it were that easy."

Her eyebrows arch. "Uh-oh. You must have an unhappy supplier or someone who is about to cut you down in a terrible business deal."

I sigh heavily. "And if it were any of those, I would know how to solve the problem."

"What's the issue?"

I picture Enzo's face, his attitude, his confidence. "I met someone last night."

Kingsley hums approvingly. "Well, I hope you sealed the deal, you dirty girl."

"Ha. I wish. He's totally hands-off."

"And why's that?

"He's the spokesperson for our new campaign. Enzo De la Rosa. Kill me now."

She waggles her finger back and forth. "And that's a no."

I nod in agreement. "A massive no. Can you imagine the headlines? 'CEO Beds Male Model Employee More Than Twenty Years Her Junior.' It would be terrible. Absolutely terrible."

She shrugs a shoulder impishly. "You could fire him."

I laugh heartily. "You know I won't do that. But, God, when I met him, it was instant attraction."

She stares at me with *that's obvious* written in her eyes. "He *is* a stunning supermodel."

I shake my head, because that's not the issue. "It wasn't his looks. It was his attitude. It was the way he talked to me. The way he dripped with confidence. And that wasn't about his looks either. It was a confidence about his brain. To be that good-looking and that smart . . ." I exhale deeply, full of wishes I can't fulfill.

"And you're going to be a good girl and deny all your feelings?"

I nod solemnly; Kingsley has only validated what I'd convinced myself of already. Raising my hand, I vow, "Deny, disown, and ignore them completely."

INTERLUDE

Spencer

Ah, so we have a little chemistry brewing between Enzo and Valerie, but it seems this illicit office romance might pose more challenges than anyone suspected.

For now, though, let's leave behind our couple pretending to be less and check back in with our friends pretending to be more.

Just a refresher—Gavin has just asked Savannah to play the role of his fake girlfriend.

This should be interesting.

Because pretend romances *always* go as planned.

They never become complicated by things like —*gasp*— feelings that surprise the fuck out of you.

10

GAVIN

I adjust my button-down in the mirror, run a hand through my dark hair, and give myself a thumbs-up.

"It's a little shocking to see myself in something other than a T-shirt, but I do rock a dress shirt," I announce to the crowd of one.

"Dude, you look like a billionaire!" Eddie calls out from the couch. "They wear buttons all the time."

I arch a brow. "Buttons? That's the hallmark of a rich dude?"

"Yes. Obviously." He flubs his lips as he searches my Netflix queue on his laptop. "I read all those books. Including the ones from a few years back with the alien billionaire in blue." Eddie stares at the ceiling. "Now that I think about it, I haven't seen that model in a while."

"You remember models on book covers?"

"Leggy Lisa liked him. I made the effort to learn more about her hobbies."

I laugh, shaking my head at him. "Remind me again why you're on my couch? You don't even live here."

He pats the well-worn cushions. Well-worn from his ass parked on them all the time. "'Cause your place is awesome. You don't mind if I crash here, do you?"

"No. But what if I did?" I ask rhetorically.

"Then we'd sit down and have a sesh, bro. We'd talk it out. Find some common ground."

"Excellent. Just making sure you had a strategy."

He taps his forehead. "I'm always thinking. And right now, I'm thinking you need to have some fucking fun tonight, man. You haven't had much since you broke up with Denise."

"Correction—since Denise broke up with me."

He shakes his head vehemently. "I don't see it that way. Sure, technically, it went down like that. But I like to think you broke up with her. Because that's what you should have done months before. Like, right after you started up with her. She was no good for you."

I shoot him a curious glance. "Why is that?"

"Because she wasn't fun. She wasn't funny. And she wasn't friends with you."

I consider his assessment. Maybe he's onto something. "So you're saying it was never right with her?"

"Never. I mean, she didn't even laugh when I told her about the toilet plunger named Fred that I had to carry to work one day. And, admit it, that was best-story-ever level. Savannah cracked up when I told her about Fred."

Eddie works for a company that shoots industrial videos for tradesmen. I smile, remembering Savannah's reaction the night Eddie waxed on and on about his boss requesting he pick up a plunger for a photo shoot.

"Savannah did appreciate the story of Fred, true. She has a good sense of humor if she can tolerate you."

He smirks. "Exactly." Then he points to the door. "Now, get the hell out of here. Have a good time with the Sav-meister. I'm going to watch some Netflix on your TV."

"Enjoy my place."

He winks. "I always do."

As I walk through the neighborhood on my way to meet Savannah, I think back on the last two years of working together, hanging out together, going to see music together, and grabbing a bite for lunch together. We were total buds, and I loved our friendship. But when Denise came into my life nine months ago, Savannah and I didn't do as much of that any longer. Understandably, Denise didn't want me hanging out with another woman.

Come to think of it, I did miss Savannah's company for a while there. She's lighthearted, easygoing, and we always have something to talk about.

Good thing I won't have to worry about Denise's opinion tonight. Eddie's right on that count.

I head into the neighborhood bar to meet Savannah and work on our backstory. When I see her, seated on a barstool, her hair flowing past her shoulders, something hits me for the very first time.

Why have I never noticed how pretty she is?

Oh, right, because we've only been friends. And I had a girlfriend part of that time. And I'm a good guy and not an asshole, so I didn't have eyes for other women. But now that I'm not with Denise, all I see are Savannah's toned legs, her long hair, and those big blue eyes.

Holy shit, is my closest female friend a total babe and I never noticed it until tonight?

It's possible. It's highly possible indeed.

I walk up to her, clear my throat, and feel more awkward than I've ever felt before with her. "So, how long have we been going out?" I say, diving right into the reason we're here.

She laughs. "Good to see you too."

"Hey. Sorry. Also, you look nice."

I want to say *You look pretty*, because she does.

Only I don't, because all these thoughts are colliding at once and I need to figure them out.

She glances down at her outfit—simple jeans and a pink top. "Thanks, and I think we should say we've been dating for three months. Because that's enough time where you might not have told your mom about me but not so much time that it will seem crazy."

"And what do we like to do for fun?" I ask, after I order a beer.

"We like to play bocce ball," she says, rattling off an activity that we've done a few times in the past. "We love to go see musicians play. And we definitely, really, totally dig trying to eat the spiciest food in all of Manhattan."

A grin spreads easily on my face. "Hey, it sounds like it's not even a fake story."

She flashes me a smile. "There's nothing fake at all about that story."

And the funny thing is, it doesn't feel the least bit fake to me either. It doesn't feel fake to me when I pay for our beer or when we walk to the party. It doesn't feel fake to me when I loop an arm around her waist as we stroll along the streets of Brooklyn.

And it doesn't feel fake at all when there's the slightest tremble from her as I touch her.

We get to the engagement party and everything feels ridiculously, incredibly real. Everything comes into focus at last. It's as if I wore the opposite of rose-colored glasses around her, and they blurred her from the realm of possibility. Now the glasses are off, and I can see clearly what's been right in front of me all along.

We grab two beers from the waiter, and I hand her one first.

She tips the bottle to mine and says, "Cheers," and even that word feels different, like we have something to cheer about.

When that new girl band we signed plays on the

sound system, I point to the speaker. "One of your favorites," I say. "The Violet Rays rock."

Her smile ignites instantly. "I love their music. And their lyrics hit me in the heart every time."

"Yeah, why's that?" I'm soaking up every detail, learning the inside story of Savannah for the first time, it seems.

"Because they're so honest. They talk about love and heartache, about being broken but then overcoming it."

I raise my bottle, toasting again. "To overcoming heartbreak."

"I will definitely drink to that."

The conversation rolls from one topic to the next as we catch up on stories in the news, places we dig in the neighborhood, and whether Glass Slipper should institute a bring-your-dog-to-work-every-day rule. We decide dogs in the office would be dope.

We've had convos like this before, but everything feels different now. I can't believe I didn't see her as more than a friend before Denise, but I definitely see her that way now.

Soon, my mom joins us and asks us the questions we prepped for. How long we've been together, how we met, and so on.

"You are such a delightful couple," my mother declares, beaming between us with the hope that can only stir up that quickly in a mom. "So what's next for you two?"

Savannah clasps a hand around my arm. "Gavin and I just like to have fun together. That's all we're thinking about for now."

That effectively shuts off the questions from my mom, which is exactly what I wanted for tonight.

And exactly what I no longer want.

Because now that I'm seeing this woman in a new light, I'm seeing us moving out of the friend zone and into a zone I didn't think I was ready to enter.

When I walk her home, I clear my throat and say, "Thank you for being my fake date. But I have a confession to make."

She stops, tilts her head, and meets my gaze. "What is it?"

I jump into the deep end. No point doing anything else. "Not a thing about it felt fake."

There's a hint of nerves when she asks, "What do you mean, Gavin?"

For the last two years, I've been missing what's right in front of me. Missing it because we were just friends, then missing it because I was involved, and lately, missing it because it simply didn't occur to me.

But now, Savannah *has* occurred to me, and I don't want to waste any more time.

"What I mean is, if I kissed you right now, I'd like it to be a real kiss," I say, and her eyes seem to dance with starlight. "What do you think about that, Savannah?"

The smile that crosses her face is magnetic. "I think you should really kiss me."

It's the best response in the history of questions and answers.

11

GAVIN

I slide a hand across her face, and she trembles as my thumb strokes her cheek.

A small rush of air escapes her lips, as if she's sighing into the possibility of a touch. I move closer and press a soft kiss to her mouth, figuring soft and subtle is the way to start.

She seems to like it that way, and so do I. It works for a little bit, this gentle exploration, as I experience the flavor of her kiss.

But soon, I find myself wanting more of her, and the kiss darts up to another level. It's hotter, and hungrier, as my hand loops into her hair, those lush strands wrapping around my fingers.

Savannah kisses me back with fierceness and determination. I respond in kind, raising the stakes—more roughness, more heat.

Then I'm not sure if I'm kissing her or if she's kissing me. All I know is her back is up against the brick wall of her building. My hands are in her hair, and hers are sliding down my body, grabbing my ass, yanking me closer. She seals her body against mine, letting me know she wants all the same things I do. My mind takes many, many steps ahead to where this could go, to what we could be.

In a heartbeat, her hands are on my chest, and she pushes me away.

I look at her, dazed. "Is everything okay?"

She nods, a little breathless. "I'm okay."

"Are you sure? Because you just shoved me away. Generally speaking, that means you don't want to kiss me anymore."

She sighs and runs a hand through her hair. "I do want to. But I'm going to be totally honest. I don't think you're ready for it. And I also don't want to ruin what we have." She takes a deep breath like she's prepping herself for something hard. "I think we need to focus on being friends."

I try to reroute thoughts already racing ahead to what we could be next. But maybe she's onto something. Maybe this is the way to demonstrate I'm not rushing into anything post-breakup. "So if we focus on being friends, would that prove to you how I really feel?"

She tilts her face. Her lips are soft; her eyes are vulnerable. "I don't know. How *do* you really feel?"

I drag my thumb along her jawline, and she closes her eyes as if it's almost too much. And then I speak the complete and utter truth. "I'm just beginning to figure it out tonight."

She opens her eyes. There's a certainty in her gaze. "That's exactly why we need to continue being friends."

* * *

Later, when I'm alone, I wonder if I've been friend-zoned. And then I decide I shouldn't be asking myself. I should ask *her*. I send her a text.

Gavin: Was that a friend-zoning?

Savannah: Did it feel like a friend-zoning?

Gavin: I have no idea.

Savannah: Do you want to be friend-zoned?

Gavin: I think I made it clear that I don't want that.

Savannah: Let's consider it a temporary measure.

Gavin: So I can eventually get a zoning change?

Savannah: Maybe. :) What zone are you trying to get into?

Gavin: I thought that was abundantly clear tonight. I want to get into the end zone with you.

Savannah: And I thought you were the music guy. All of a sudden, you can't stop with the sports analogies. :)

Gavin: Sports analogies seem to work well in this case.

Savannah: Yes, so let me be as clear as a fifty-yard touchdown pass into the end zone—I don't *just* want to sleep with you.

Gavin: Allow me to be as clear as a game-winning home run—I don't just want to sleep with you either.

I re-read the text, and it feels like one of the truest things I've ever written. To anyone.

But I also know that I need to prove myself to her. That's why I send one more text.

Gavin: How about a game of bocce ball this weekend?

Savannah: I thought you'd never ask.

12

GAVIN

As I toss the ball along the lawn, I ask her more questions, diving into all the things I don't know about her. I know a lot already, but there's so much uncharted territory too. I ask about her family, her mother, her aunt Ellen.

"This may shock you, since I'm not a traditional gal, but Aunt Ellen is—very much so—and I adore her. She's this sweet, darling old lady, and she loves to crochet," Savannah says, a lightness in her tone as she talks about her family.

"Is that why you know how to crochet?" I ask after she throws the ball.

The look she gives me brims with curiosity. "How did you know I know how to crochet?"

"Was it a secret?"

She shrugs, a little impishly. "I don't go out and advertise it." She whispers, "It's not very Brooklyn hipster."

I pat her shoulder, taking advantage of any chance I get to touch her. "Aw. Don't worry. Your Brooklyn hipster cred is still good with me. Crocheting is super retro." I loop an arm around her waist and pull her close.

She arches a brow. "Is that friendly?"

I hold up my free hand in surrender. "Seems completely friendly to me."

"It's not making me think friendly thoughts," she whispers.

I grin. "Excellent."

"You're being bad," she says, but her tone is playful. "But let's get back to the topic. How did you know I like to crochet?"

I grab another ball and send it down the grass. Then I turn to her, admitting, "I spotted crochet hooks in your bag once. Thought it was kind of adorable."

She acts shocked. "You little spy. And you knew they were crochet hooks instead of knitting needles or something else?"

"Um. Confession: I did. I was raised by the latest in a long line of crafty women."

"Excellent. Crafty women are forces of good in the world."

"I'd have to agree," I say, as she defeats me for the twentieth time, it seems. "Also, I was not thinking friendly thoughts as I watched you throw that ball."

She rolls her eyes, but that feels like a good sign.

* * *

At the end of the friendly date, I walk her home again. I'm tempted to kiss her on the front steps of her apartment building, but I also am keenly aware I'm on a mission to show her that I listened. That we can be friends first.

The next weekend we see a new band, but I can't say we stay completely in the friend zone at the club. There might be more touches than usual as the music thrums. She might put her arm around me as the band slides into a guitar riff that radiates in my bones. And when they're done and we head to a nearby bar, I take her hand.

I glance down at our hands as we walk. "So how about this? Is this friendly?"

She chuckles. "I hold hands with my friends all the time."

"You better not hold hands with any guy friends."

Her expression shifts to serious. "Gavin, do you really think we're acting like friends?"

I nod, maintaining a straight face. "I do. We're acting like such good friends that I'll let you buy me a beer."

She nudges me with her elbow. "I'm not buying you a beer."

"Hey! That's what friends do. I'm just saying."

"No, friends would go dutch."

"Fine. We'll go dutch."

* * *

At the bar, the touchy, flirty vibe continues over beers, until she leans in close, a little breathy, a little frisky, and says, "If I have another one, I will probably grab your face and kiss you like crazy."

A groan rumbles up my chest. I raise a hand as if talking to the bartender. "One more for the lady."

She shakes her head, stands, and parks a hand on my shoulder. "I need to go or I'm going to do something I'll regret."

I want her to kiss me like crazy, but I don't want her to regret a damn thing.

Once more, I walk her home. This time it's even tougher to resist kissing her. To resist asking to go up. Instead, I ask a question. "Why would you regret what you might do?"

A deep sigh crosses her lips and her eyes flash with vulnerability. "I don't want to be a rebound girl."

Softly, I ask, "What do you want to be, Savannah?"

"I want to be more than a rebound." She points her thumb at the door. "And on that note, I really need to go inside."

As she heads inside and I go home, all I can think is she doesn't feel like a rebound girl.

She feels like the complete opposite. The one that stays.

13

SAVANNAH

Two months later, we're out testing some new burgers at a place that offers fifty different flavors of sauces, including at least a dozen in the "fiery" category. Translation: my kind of place.

We opt for a sampler of burger bites, showing off our "I can hold my spice better than you" chops. I bite into one with red-hot jalapeño and smile as I eat the inferno.

He takes a chance with a ghost pepper burger, and even as a bead of sweat breaks out on his forehead, he remains stoic.

It's adorable.

I love how tough he is about something so pointless but so damn fun.

I opt for the spiciest possible burger—a red chili style—and take a bite.

Oh, holy mother of fiery food.

Smoke forms inside my head. My tongue goes up

in five-alarm flames.

I wave my hand in front of my face. I cough, and Gavin thrusts me a glass of water. I down it quickly. "Are you okay?" he asks.

"I think I've hit my limit," I choke.

"Will you live though?"

Another cough bursts from my throat. "It's debatable."

A few glasses of water and slices of bread later, I'm alive and mostly well.

He straightens his shoulders and wiggles his brows. "So it's safe to say I win?"

I narrow my eyes. "Grrr. Yes. That's the spiciest thing I've ever eaten."

He raises his hands in victory. "Behold the Spicinator."

"You won, but I am not getting you a T-shirt," I protest. "And I'm not crocheting you a blanket either."

"That's cool. I have bragging rights, and that's what I wanted." He inches a little closer to me in the booth. "Hey, do you know what the best way is to get rid of that spicy sensation?"

Curious, I answer, "I don't. What *is* the best way to get rid of an intensely spicy sensation?"

"You need to be kissed."

A little shiver of pleasure spreads across my skin. "So you want to kiss away the residual red chili in my mouth?"

"I'm totally open to that."

I laugh. But then I stop laughing. Because it's two

months later and we're still doing this. We're still being friends, doing all the things we've done before, working together, hanging out, and having fun.

When we leave the restaurant, I take his hand, something we've done a lot lately.

But this time, it feels vastly different.

He looks down at our hands, then back at me, his eyes flashing with promise. "Is that what friends do?"

I shake my head. "No, and friends don't invite friends to spend the night."

INTERLUDE

Spencer

Told you so.

I mean, not to be cocky, but I called that from a mile away.

Fake dates? *C'mon.*

Been there, done that, have the wedding ring to prove it.

Still, there are plenty of pitfalls on the path from a fake date to a sleepover. It's a slippery slope from the friend zone to the bedroom zone.

But hey, maybe they like it slippery.

That's hardly the only tricky ground friends and lovers might encounter.

Coworkers too. I bet they face some very rocky terrain as the former blue alien billionaire must confront a thorny issue.

14

ENZO

I give my best smoldering look to the right of the lens.

The photographer calls out. "Nice. If you look directly at the camera, we will all melt from the intensity of your gaze."

He is too kind.

A small smile tickles my lips, and the snap of the lens confirms the photographer captures that too. "Brilliant. You look great when you're smiling."

"Enzo looks fantastic when he smiles, and when he doesn't smile, and every other time too."

It's the woman from the art gallery. The CEO of Wu Media and the most captivating woman I've ever met. I've only spent a few minutes in Valerie's company, but I'm already enthralled. "I can give you a more serious look if you want," I offer, since I want to please her.

"Just keep doing what you're doing," the photographer says.

"Yes, everything you're doing is perfect," Valerie adds.

I follow the photographer's instructions as he captures more shots, trying desperately to keep my eyes off the gorgeous woman, even as she sings my praises.

"That's going to position Wu Media incredibly well. My advertising team will be so incredibly pleased with this."

"Your team will be satisfied. Is that so?" I say when the shooting stops and the photographer steps away to grab a coffee.

Valerie meets my gaze, adding pointedly, "Yes, *satisfied.*"

"And what about you, Valerie?" My question is suggestive, playing off the last word she said.

She's quiet at first, as if she's schooling her expression, then she asks in a most professional voice, "What about me?"

I arch a brow. "What would it take for you to be satisfied?"

"Oh, I'm a very difficult woman in that regard," she says, keeping that cool, composed tone.

Hmm. Perhaps I read her wrong at the gallery, but I don't think so. One more shot.

"I would be up to that challenge."

She closes her eyes, takes a breath, and then opens them again. "This can't happen. *We* can't happen. I hope I'm not being presumptuous in saying that."

That's what I want to hear and what I don't want

to hear at all. "You're not being presumptuous, because I want little more in the world than for *this* to happen. But why can't it? Do you not let *that* happen here in your country?" I ask playfully, as if I'm unfamiliar with her customs.

She laughs, and the sound is so seductive and sensual. "Oh, no, we love it when *that* happens."

"Then why can't *we* happen? You and I had an instant connection when we met, didn't we?"

"Oh, we certainly did," she says in nearly a whisper. "Too much of one."

"There is no such thing. So then, if we both feel that same pull, why not?" I have to know. I must understand the barriers.

She straightens her shoulders. "It's because I'm head of this company and you're a contractor. If word got out that we had a dalliance, it would be terrible for me."

All the air rushes from me, knocked out by the perfect sense of her point. "I see. That makes me terribly sad." But I made my way out of the slums. I am a determined man and determined to find a way to her heart. "But perhaps we could be friends."

"Friends?" she asks as if she's tasting a new dish, something foreign but perhaps something she finds enticing.

"Friends," I say, low and smoky, then make my true intentions clear. "It is a thing that people do when they enjoy spending time with each other but they don't fuck."

Her eyes darken.

"You like that idea?" I step closer, not to the point of impropriety, but close enough that I see the goose-bumps dusting her skin. "You like it when I say 'fuck,' don't you?"

Her shoulders shudder, but then she seems to center herself. "Of course I do. I like it when you say anything to me. But that is my point. We can't happen. So I have to walk away."

She spins on her heel and leaves, making me more determined than ever to see her walking toward me someday soon.

15

VALERIE

A few weeks later, there's a knock on my office door, and Sadie pops in. "You received an invitation from Highsmith Associates. Private auction. All the proceeds go to charity."

My eyebrows rise. "What charity? And what sort of artwork?"

"It's an organization that provides college scholarships in the United States for children of immigrants."

I nod approvingly. I know something about that cause. Sadie rattles off the names of the artists, and they all delight me, especially when she mentions Hunter Edmonds, a rising star in the art world.

"Daniel at Highsmith wanted to personally invite you. He's only extending the invitation to a few premium buyers, he said—those who love art and doing good. Someone gave him your name as a collector who'd want to attend."

She gives me the time and the date, and even

though I'm swimming in deals and partnerships, I know I'll go. For the cause, and for the art.

* * *

I put on my best black dress and make my way to Highsmith, where I take a paddle and head to the front row. Moments later, the man I walked away from at the gallery arrives and sits next to me, smelling like the ocean breeze and looking like he just stepped out of a magazine shoot.

Because he probably did.

"Fancy meeting you here," I muse.

"What a surprise indeed," he says, all cool and sexy.

I shoot him an inquisitive glance. "Are you here to bid on the art?"

He gives a laid-back shrug. "Why else would I be here?"

"I don't know."

"Well, you are correct. For that, and to work on the friendship, of course. I had a feeling you'd enjoy this auction."

"And that's why you arranged for an invite?"

"Did I do that?" he asks playfully.

I shoot him a *you're so naughty* grin. "Are we working on a friendship, Enzo?"

"Yes. If friendship entails a little friendly bidding on art, can't we? I bet you'll enjoy the thrill of the chase."

"I bet I will."

The auction begins, and Enzo raises his paddle, making the opening bid when a Hunter Edmonds goes on sale. When I bid higher, he keeps going, lifting the paddle and elevating the stakes. He glances at me. "I bet you'd enjoy other uses for paddles."

I gasp, even as sparks race across my skin. "You're a filthy man."

"But am I wrong?"

I square my shoulders. "I'm not going to tell you."

"Valerie," he chides, "that's not friendly."

"I didn't think it was a friendly question at all," I say, but I'm reining in a dirty grin.

He affects a most innocent expression. "I only meant it in a friendly way. As one friend inquiring about what the other likes."

I point at the painting. "What I would like is to acquire that Edmonds. For the cause, of course. And for my wall."

"Then I will make it so."

And he makes the bid so ridiculous, so over-the-top, so absolutely grandiose that even the huntress in me must acquiesce.

* * *

When the auction ends, he asks the auctioneer to wrap it up and then he brings it to me. "Consider it a gift from one friend to another."

"Before I can take it," I say as I put a hand on his arm, "are you saying this because you want to be friends with me or because you want to take me to bed?"

"You underestimate yourself," he says. It's a growl, masculine and carnal.

"I hardly ever do that."

He cups my cheek. "I don't just want to fuck you. And I don't just want to be your friend. I want more."

I tremble at his forwardness. My heart and my body want to give in. But my head knows better. "But we can't have more. I've worked hard to be where I am. I've built this company myself from the ground up. And I need to take care of it and my employees."

"I know. I do understand. Your reputation matters. I respect you too much, and that's why I will leave you here with this most friendly of unfriendly thoughts." He steps closer, his soulful eyes locked with my gaze. "I want to kiss you. I want to touch you. I want to fuck you all night long. I want to make love to you in the morning. And I want to spend the day with you." He exhales. "But I understand your wishes, and I respect that we can't do that, so now, I must insist that we remain friends."

I shiver as I answer. "Yes."

It is the hardest yes I've ever had to give.

* * *

Enzo calls me the next day at work.

"Just calling as a friend," he says.

I don't have time to chat, but that's what we do.

He asks me how I started Wu Media. I tell him how I won a scholarship for college in the United States, then for graduate school in business, and how I grew the company to where it is today. It took long hours, intense focus, and fierce dedication.

"I imagine it's the same for you," I say. "I've read articles about your background. You worked hard to break into the business."

"I did, and I want to keep working hard every day. In fact, I just booked a job with Gigante. To be the new face of the brand."

I laugh, sensing an opportunity to tease him. "Enzo, I'm not so sure it's your face they're after."

He laughs too. "No? You think it's something else? My, how do you say it, booty?"

"Yes. I imagine they like that quite a bit. And now I'm imagining you modeling underwear, and that's simply unfair. You can't plant these pictures in my head."

"Where should I plant them?" he asks ever so innocently.

"In a garden. In the backyard."

"Ah, of course. I'll work on watering a garden of naughty images for you."

"We're friends," I remind him. "Just friends."

"Ah, right. Of course. Then, as a friend, would you like to attend a private showing of the new Miller Valentina collection at the Blue Light Gallery?"

My heart skips a beat. I twirl the phone cord and kick my heel back and forth. There is something delicious about old-school phones. They're excellent for playing with when it comes to flirting.

Except flirting is what I really shouldn't do with him. "Let's see. Miller Valentina, as in one of the most coveted modern artists?"

"The one and only Miller Valentina," he says. "How did I know you would be a fan of his?"

It's not a question. It's a statement. Even so, I turn it around on him because I'm intensely curious. "Yes, how *did* you know?"

"Because you're a woman of discerning taste. And he is one of the finest artists of our generation. I took a stab. Was I right?"

I kick my high-heeled foot back and forth. "I am indeed a woman of discerning taste."

He hums. It's an enticing sound, especially because it's almost as if he hums with an accent. "Yes, you do have excellent taste."

Butterflies seem to swoop in my chest, a sensation I haven't felt in years. It's not as if I've put matters of the body on the back burner. It's that running this business can be all-consuming, so I haven't had time to feel a thing for anyone for years. But I feel something for this man who is so persistent and who seems to know me so well, from my motivation to make something of myself to my taste in art. "I've been in love with Valentina's work for some time. I assume you can handle my adoration of him?"

Enzo seems utterly amused. "Not only can I

handle it, but I look forward to seeing you delight in his work. As a friend, of course."

There's a wink in his voice, and I grin from the other side of the city. "Yes. As a friend. Since we are friends."

"We are *only* friends," he says with a note of longing.

It feels a little sad, but I'm hopeful at the same time too, as if we've found this terrific loophole and we plan to exploit it.

* * *

I don't doll myself up as if it were a date. But I do make sure I look absolutely fabulous a few days later when I find him waiting outside the gallery, looking head-to-toe lickable in charcoal slacks and a polo shirt that shows off his terrifically toned arms.

His eyes roam over me, eating me up. I've never felt so wanted in my life. Dropping a kiss onto one cheek then the other, he whispers in a husky voice, "I'm only saying this as a friend, but you look absolutely stunning."

I give him a lingering once-over. "You're not too bad yourself."

He holds open the door. I go inside, and he follows me, his hand barely dusting the small of my back as he guides me to a painting he wants me to see.

It takes my breath away.

It's overwhelming, the kind of canvas that takes up

more than an entire wall with its size and stature. Twelve panels of people kissing, pop art kisses, all of them making my damn heart flutter.

Enzo leans closer to me, whispering, "Those kisses? What do you think of them?"

"I think they're incredibly alluring," I say, my voice feathery, then I look at him. "And not in a friendly way at all. You're so sneaky."

He brings a hand to his chest as if affronted. "You assume I'm sending you subliminal messages?" He wags a finger at me. "Such a naughty woman."

I run my thumb along his cheekbone. "I would never assume such a thing. Not with such an innocent face."

"I do have an innocent face at times. But I'm not so innocent."

"I doubt you're innocent at all."

He sets a hand on my elbow, making my skin sizzle. "Let's go look at more art," he suggests, and it sounds like foreplay.

Perhaps it is.

Over the next few weeks, he takes me to more galleries, more shows, more museums, knowing this is my weakness, this is what delights me. Or maybe it's simply that *he* delights me.

As we wander the halls, we talk, and I learn about his life growing up in Madrid and what brought him to this country. I share my stories too, telling him about where I was born and raised in Shanghai and what lured me to America—schooling and opportunity.

"We're not that different," he muses as we wander through the Cloisters.

"I suppose we're not. Both rising up, making something of ourselves from humble beginnings."

He nods. "We are bootstrappers."

I smile, loving that word, then I decide to take a bigger risk. After all, my stomach is rumbling. "I'm starving."

"What are you in the mood for? I can check the Michelin app for a fantastic restaurant, or we can go to that new sushi place that everyone's raving about."

I wiggle a brow and lower my voice. "Pizza. I want pizza. This is New York after all. And aren't you becoming a New Yorker?"

"I am indeed, and I read somewhere once that a New Yorker folds his pizza."

"A New Yorker definitely folds a slice of 'za."

"Let's go fold some slices, Valerie."

We head to the nearest Famous Ray's, where I order two cheese slices. We stand at the counter, chowing down on our folded pizzas, watching the city go by, and sharing more stories of life, then and now.

I rather like my *now*.

I like it a lot.

When we're done, I clear my throat, drawing up all

my confidence. "I have to go shopping next week for a gift. It's my good friend Kingsley's birthday, and I have a bit of a dilemma."

He tilts his chin. "I love dilemmas. How can I help you solve it?"

"I like to get chocolate or cake as gifts for my friends. But Kingsley runs a chocolate company."

"You can't get her chocolate. We need to find something else for your friend."

"I know. But what? Every year I try to find something new for her. Cupcakes. Old-fashioned sweets. Last year I even sent her Famous Ray's, since she, too, is a woman of excellent taste who loves pizza."

"Never trust someone who doesn't like pizza," he says, his lips quirking into a grin.

"Exactly. But I can't do pizza again this year."

He taps his chin, thinking. "Wait. I know. I've always loved macarons."

I grin at the perfection of his answer, and at the idea it sparks. "Perhaps you'd like to shop with me? Since I'm helping a friend, of course."

"And I'll help you. My wonderful new friend." His smile is devilish and not the least bit friendly.

Everything about the shopping date feels risky, but it feels like a risk I can't keep from taking.

16

ENZO

A man should always be early when he is courting a woman. Of course, I'm pretending it's not courting, but I can't fool myself.

In my mind, I am absolutely courting her.

After I meet my agent to discuss the next phase of a campaign, I make my way to the macaron shop on the Upper East Side, planning to arrive early.

I stop at a crosswalk as the light turns yellow. A blonde woman hurries to cross the street from the other side, and just as she reaches the curb and sees me, she does a double take and stumbles.

Into a manhole.

Instinct kicks in, and I rush over, grabbing her waist before she drops all the way down.

She gasps as I pull her up to safety. "Oh my God, you saved my life."

"I couldn't let you fall."

She raises a hand in front of her face, breathing hard. "I think I already have."

"Let me help you to the sidewalk," I say, steadying her until she recovers her footing.

"I was ogling you, I must confess."

"Then it's all the better that I rescued you, because we can't have you die from ogling. I hear that's a terrible way to go," I say with a wry grin.

"You are too kind. Please, will you have drinks with me tonight? Maybe I can ogle you safely then?"

I shake my head. "I am honored that you asked. But I'm a taken man."

When I arrive at the macaron shop, I'm already late. I find Valerie quickly, and she arches a brow. "Forgive me for my tardiness," I say, then tell her what happened.

She studies me quizzically. "You saved a woman who was staring at you?"

"I did."

She shakes her head as if amazed. "You are too much. I bet you made her day."

"And then she asked me out."

Valerie's shoulders tense, her whole body stiffening. "What did you say?"

I smile at her, grinning like I have a secret. "I said that I'm a taken man."

She studies me, then asks, "Are you?"

I nod, confident in my choice. "I am."

"Who is this woman?"

I move in close, brushing her dark hair behind her

ear then whispering, "This woman who says we're only friends."

She shivers, another telltale sign that I'm breaking her down. She swallows then, and it seems to clear her head. "Have an orange blossom macaron. It tastes like heaven melting on your tongue."

She offers it to me, but I don't take it with my hands. I lean in and take it off her fingers with my lips, holding her gaze the whole time. "I love dessert," I tell her after I finish it.

"You look too good eating it."

"I bet I look better eating other sweet things."

Her eyes widen in mock surprise. "You're very naughty. And you're making me think very unfriendly things."

I slide my hand down her back. "Good. Then it is working."

She turns to me, that serious expression on her face again. "It is working. It's working all too well, and it's becoming too dangerous. As much as I want this, we can't while we're working together. And if I see you again, I fear I might cross a line I shouldn't."

When the shopping ends, I fear, too, that this is the last I'll see of the woman I'm falling for.

She can't risk the ruin of her reputation.

And I can't keep asking her to.

17

ENZO

Frustrated, I head to a bar that night, enjoying the 1920s Great Gatsby theme, and sit at the counter, perusing the drink specials.

When the bartender sets down a cocktail napkin, she declares, "You look like you need something to quench your frustration."

I shove a hand through my hair. "Is it that obvious?"

"Bartender special talent. Something isn't going your way?"

I heave a sigh. "That's one way of putting it. There is a woman."

She smiles. "When a man is frustrated, it's usually about a woman."

I sigh, thinking of Valerie. "I saw her again this afternoon. I even asked her out on a date. But she said we couldn't be involved if I'm working with her, which I am. And until I no longer work with her, I can't have her the way I want to have her."

"You could quit," she offers, mixing my drink.

Perhaps she's onto something.

INTERLUDE

Spencer

Well, lookee there.

It seems all sorts of couples think they can be just friends.

But can a relationship that ignores half your feelings ever last? Do you flip the switch of desire from on to off and focus on friendship only, like Enzo and Valerie are trying to do? Or do you dial up the heat from friends to lovers?

Many have tried.

Many have failed.

But not all.

Which brings me back to my pals Jason and Truly. There might have been a bit of instant attraction that first night, but they're both grown-ups and they've been able to table it with no problem at all for a few years now.

What? You don't believe me? Then maybe it's time to check in and see exactly how they're doing.

18

TRULY

Like a soldier running drills, I take the next leg of the obstacle course, alternating jumps in tires then leaping over a plank.

Jason remains right by my side then lunges for the rope ahead. "Faster, faster, faster," I encourage him.

"Woman, I'm going as fast as I can," he says in that yummy voice that entertains me so much. We climb down the rope and reach the end of the course before anyone else in the class. I raise a hand to high-five my teammate.

"We are killing it," I say, panting.

"That is because you are absolutely ferocious. I'm terrified. Have I mentioned that before?"

"Only every time we work out together."

That's become our thing in the last few years since we met. After punk rope, we couldn't stop. We signed up for everything, from bike races to mud races and even jujitsu.

It's funny because the first night I met Jason, I was wildly attracted to him for those five minutes at the bar. And look, he's a handsome-as-hell guy. But I quickly shut down those romantic notions, and now we've segued into this wonderful friendship.

A friendship that I love and cherish. A friendship that I don't want to do a damn thing to destroy.

Because now, not only is Jason's relationship with my brother at stake, but so is mine.

I like him as a friend, and I want to keep him in my life. And I see him as part of my life, an important member of my social circle. So I don't think of him romantically anymore.

I simply don't.

When we finish class, we make our way to Chelsea.

"Hey, I had an idea for your bar," he offers. "What if you did signature drinks that you named?"

Color me intrigued. "Go on."

"I was thinking you could make up recipes, give them fun names, and maybe give each of them a story."

My brain whirs, immediately latching onto the concept. "That's kind of a brilliant idea. Like, I could do Hush Money and devise a little story about the drink you need when you have to keep something quiet."

"Another could be Last Word, and you'd tell a tale about getting the final word in."

"Or Devil's Teeth, and that's the drink for when

you've made a daring escape." I beam at him as we turn the corner toward Gin Joint. "You're brilliant."

"Nope. You are a wildly clever bar mistress."

I give him the side-eye. "I think it was you who just came up with that idea."

"Then I am wildly clever too."

"Obviously, the way you seem to juggle everything." I shift gears. "Speaking of, how are all your endeavors going?"

As an entrepreneur, Jason keeps irons in both the best-man-for-hire world and the men's advice one too. "Soon I'm going to have guys coming into my bar asking, 'Do you happen to know a best man for hire?' And I'll say, 'I'll tell you. He's the *best* best man in all of Manhattan.'"

His amber eyes twinkle. "Yes, that's exactly what I want. I can picture it now."

"And when they ask for grooming tips or dating tips or job tips, I'll reference you too. I'll say, 'Have you read it in The Modern Gentleman in New York? Because I have.'" I pause for a second, then add, "I've been enjoying your column. You should do one on how men and women can indeed be friends."

"And wherever would I find the perfect example?"

"Hello? Us! Every day."

He draws a breath as if he's weighing my suggestion. "So you want me to do a column on how men and women can be friends? What would I say in it?"

I tap my finger against my lips, diving into the idea well. "You say, 'Find common interests, find things to talk about, and then make sure to make time for each other.'"

"Seems we do all that. We're the poster children."

When we reach Gin Joint, he says goodbye and walks away.

As he leaves, I feel a strange pang in my chest.

What the hell?

Am I missing him already?

I've never missed a friend quite like this before.

Well, there's a first time for everything.

19

JASON

A few weeks later, Truly and I wander through Central Park, passing a playground where schoolkids scamper up the monkey bars.

"What were you like as a kid?" I ask, tipping my forehead toward the cluster of children.

"Hellion," she says. "I was a total hellion."

I shoot her a look. "I have a hard time believing that. You don't seem like you could have been a hellion at all."

She stares sharp knives at me. "How can you say that? I'm complete hellion material."

"Okay, prove it. What did you do that was so hellion-esque?"

She holds up a finger as if to make a point. "I threatened to run away once. I packed a lunch. I told my mom that I was leaving and was going to live down by the river."

"And did you go?"

"For about an hour. I had a picnic. It was quite good."

I laugh as we meander down a path. "You are so not a hellion."

She lifts her chin and gives me a defiant look. "But I wanted to be one."

I arch a skeptical brow. "Admit it. Deep down, you were a good girl."

She offers me a smile. "I was mostly good. Does that surprise you?"

"You're a mostly good girl now, so the answer is no."

"What about you? Were you a good boy?"

I square my shoulders, acting all proud. "I was a choirboy."

"You were never a choirboy."

I raise my right hand. "I was. I swear. Mum and Dad were regular churchgoers when they were together. I sang in front of the congregation as soon as I could walk."

Her lips curve in a grin. "That's actually adorable. And I bet that's where some of your confidence in speaking in front of crowds stems from."

"You may be right," I say as the path spills out to Fifth Avenue. I look at my watch. "Speaking of speaking, I need to practice a best-man speech for a wedding I'm working this weekend."

"Come by the bar once the bride and groom are hitched."

Loving the free and easy way she invites me, I give an equally easy answer. "I'll be there."

And I'm looking forward to it already.

* * *

When the I dos are through, I head straight for Gin Joint. It's almost automatic these days, giving in to the draw of Truly's place, knowing I'll see friends there like Malone, Nick and Harper, Spencer and Charlotte. But most of all, *her*.

On the train, I fire off a text to Truly, asking what's on tap. She answers straightaway.

Truly: Gin. And more gin.

Jason: Obviously. Beyond that.

Truly: A chalkboard full of delicious specialty cocktails.

Jason: Hmm. Will I like any?

Truly: Sorry, I had a hard time hearing you through your doubt. What did you say?

Jason: I said I bet everything is fantastic.

Truly: That's what I thought. Because playing hard to get with my drinks will get you nowhere.

Jason: Exactly where I don't want to be.

By the time I arrive, the crew is all gone, so I head to the bar and say hi to the woman of the hour. She offers me a smile and something about it just hooks into my heart.

Who am I kidding?

It hooks into my heart and other parts too. This friendship thing is great and horrible at the same time. I want her and I can't have her, and that's for the best, but it sucks.

I settle in, focusing on chitchat rather than unmet desires. "So, tell me. What sort of advice did you give out as the world's greatest bartender tonight?"

"Well, someone came in wanting to know how to properly grow a mustache."

I slam a palm on the counter. "My column does indeed come in handy."

"Yes, I did as you suggested and told him about the Miracle-Gro."

"Perfect."

"That's my job as a bartender. To know the answers to literally everything."

"Then what's the answer to—" I'm about to say *how friends can become lovers*, but I can't go there. I can't let on—for every reason. She's become a vital part of my world. She's part of the friendship gang. And I need everything in my life to work perfectly right now. I have bills to pay, people to support. I can't simply pursue whatever falls my way.

So I glance around the bar then ask, "What's the answer to . . . the best spot in the whole world to take a crazy, wild trip?"

"Well, obviously you want to go to Antarctica," she says immediately.

I wiggle a brow as if considering this odd suggestion. "I do?"

"Of course. Don't you want to freeze all the time?"

I shudder. "Nope. Can't say that I want that whatsoever. But I do love snow."

She leans closer, whispering like she has a secret, "Then you ought to consider going snowboarding."

"Snowboarding," I say, stroking my chin as I noodle on this. "That's not a bad idea."

That seems to spark an idea for her, judging by her tone. "Maybe we should go sometime."

"I look forward to that sometime," I say, my voice a little wistful and a little full of mischief too.

Maybe we aren't talking about snowboarding at all.

20

TRULY

Six months later, the jingle bells are jingling, and I have a blast seeing my mother and spending Christmas with her, her dogs, and my brother.

We sing Christmas carols and make up random lyrics to them on the fly, open silly little gifts, then spend the day doing volunteer work as we've done for the last several years.

The next day, I return to the city and pop into Gin Joint because even during the holidays, people still like a stiff cocktail. Perhaps more so.

Though I'm busy, my world feels both full and a little empty too, because a certain someone is gone.

Jason's back in London, visiting his mom and sister, and I feel the weight of his absence in a way I didn't expect.

I don't see him every day. I don't even see him every week. But there's the idea that I *could* see him. There's the possibility. And as I head to work on the last day of December, I'm keenly aware that I've become accustomed to his face, to the very regular presence of him. He'll stop by after a wedding, grab a beer or whiskey, or just chat. He's here often, and that's not because he's a lush. It's because this is where the gang hangs out after a softball game in the summer or during one of Malone's shows in the winter.

I won't see him tonight when I host a huge 1920s-style bash. I arrive early and work my little butt off, prepping for the party.

Fifteen minutes before we're about to open, my phone pings with a message.

Jason: And a very Happy New Year to you from London!

He adds a kiss emoji.

Truly: Emojis are so not your style.

Jason: My New Year's resolution is to resign myself to the use of emojis.

Truly: I feel like you've done a column on how men shouldn't use emojis.

Jason: Ah, my heart flutters every time you tell me you read my columns. Indeed, I do refrain from emojis. But sometimes, one must give in.

I laugh when he sends another text with the eggplant emoji.

Truly: You pervert. Also, it's not midnight yet.

Jason: Well, it's midnight here, and I've had a few glasses of the good stuff.

Truly: What's that? Whiskey?

Jason: My friends from uni plied me with champagne. I'm all pissed on bubbly. Shh. Don't tell a soul.

Truly: You're a lightweight when it comes to champagne. Your secret is safe with me.

Jason: Total champagne lightweight. Yes, I'm a little pissed.

Truly: I never tire of your British charm. Even when you use terms that sound like they should mean something else.

Jason: Oh, I have loads of charm. Also, that emoji was supposed to mean something.

Truly: The eggplant one? Yeah, I know what that means.

Jason: The lips one.

Truly: It means you have lips?

Jason: It means if you were here, I would kiss you because it's New Year's.

I pause in rearranging bottles behind the bar as I reread his note. Is he for real? Would he really kiss me?

A ribbon of heat unfurls in me as I picture how his lips would coast over mine.

Truly: Is that so, Mr. Pissed on New Year's?

Jason: I absolutely would. Quite a proper New Year's kiss.

Truly: And what's a proper New Year's kiss?

Jason: Tongue. Lots and lots of tongue.

Truly: One would hope there would be tongue.

Jason: Actually, I'd brush my lips across yours and kiss you slow at first, then I'd explore your mouth, then I'd kiss you incredibly hard.

Truly: You are drunk.

Jason: I'm tipsy. But that really doesn't change my desire to kiss you.

My stomach flips. Tingles spread all over me. This is a whole new level of flirting. I want to tell him that the feeling is mutual. I want to let him know I think about kissing him on many nights, and many mornings too. Hell, I'm thinking about it now, and it's doing all sorts of crazy things to my insides. But I also know, for a million reasons and for one really important one, I can't go there. So I write back with a rather simple "Happy New Year," and I put my phone away.

When he strolls into Gin Joint two days later, I do a double-take. I point at his face. "You have a beard."

He checks over his shoulder as if there's someone behind him, then he pats his cheeks, his jaw, his chin. "What? I do?"

I laugh at his antics. "Yes. Your face is covered in the stuff. Just thought you should know."

"Well, it's a good thing somebody is telling me the truth. I wondered why everyone was staring at me." He scrubs a hand across his facial hair. "What do you think?"

I think he looks crazy hot. Manly and sexy. Good enough to kiss. And I can't entirely hold back. As I wipe down the counter, I give a little shrug. "You're hot, furry, and unfunny."

He arches a brow, studying me. "Is that so? You think I'm hot?"

I lean forward, dropping my voice. "I thought that had already been established."

"It bears reestablishing occasionally. Or, even better, frequently. Turns out I rather enjoy it." He offers me his chin. "Want to touch?"

Those flutters? They skate down my arms, sizzling and hot. Maybe because there's a bar separating us, maybe because I'm confident this won't go anywhere beyond this simple little contact, I reach across and stroke his beard. It feels good, it feels right . . . It feels like touching him is something I'm supposed to do, and that terrifies me more than I expect.

I pull my hand away and busy myself sorting glasses behind the counter. "Why did you grow it?"

"I'm doing a column on beard grooming. I need to test the products."

"Will you keep it?"

"The products?"

I shoot him a *you can't be serious* look. "The beard, silly."

He shrugs. "I don't know. You want to test it one more time and see what you think I should do?"

It's like we're talking about something else, talking around what's happening between us. "You know, just for the column and all," he adds.

"Just for the column," I lie as I stroke it again, touching him for no one but myself.

He watches me the whole time.

Then he stops, grabs my hand, and holds my wrist. "I saw my texts from New Year's. I'm so sorry."

I'm taken aback. I wasn't expecting an apology. I honestly wasn't expecting him to mention it at all. "Why are you sorry?"

"I didn't realize what I was doing."

"You didn't mean it?" I ask, then I wish I could take it back because I sound like a needy girl who requires reassurance.

He meets my gaze, his eyes blazing. "Oh, I meant it. I meant it so fucking much."

All the air rushes from my lungs. It seems impossible to breathe when he's just put that out there. "You did?"

"I just didn't mean to say it all. To make you feel uncomfortable."

I shake my head. "They didn't make me feel uncomfortable."

He studies me, peering closely at my face. "Are you sure?"

"I'm positive, Jason."

He heaves a sigh. "Even so, I won't do it again. I'll stick to the plan."

"Is there one? A plan?"

His eyes twinkle a little bit. "The plan we've always had. The plan where we don't act on the instant attraction."

21

JASON

A week later, when we finish jujitsu class and step outside the studio, the evening has painted the sky with an orange glow. Snow has started to fall, white flakes floating down from the clouds.

Truly sighs happily. "I love snow."

"Why is that?"

"It always feels peaceful, but also possible. Do you know what I mean?"

"Like anything can happen when it snows."

She meets my gaze, her eyes lighting up. "Yes. That's exactly it. It feels like all sorts of incredible things can happen because of snow. Isn't that strange?"

I shake my head as we walk through the neighborhood. "No, I don't think it's strange. Snow is sort of inherently romantic. It makes it seem as if the city is slowing down. As if it's draping a blanket over Manhattan and secrets are being told under it."

"I want to know Manhattan's secrets," she says wistfully.

And I want to have secrets with her. I want to take her back to my place while it's snowing and have all sorts of secrets that the weather will keep for us.

"You know what I also like about snow?" she asks.

"Tell me."

"Snowboarding. Weren't we going to go? Do you want to get out of the city this weekend?"

"Do I ever."

"We should invite Malone," she suggests.

But when she reaches out to him in our group chat, he says he can't go because he's busy.

I'm more relieved than I thought possible. I don't want to go snowboarding with Malone and Truly. I want to go snowboarding with *her*.

So we make a plan to get away.

As we drive toward the mountains in a rental car that weekend, we blast Rolling Stones and sing "Wild Horses" and then croon "Come Together" by the Beatles. We can't resist belting out Eric Clapton's "Layla" either.

"Nothing is better than singing classic rock with you. Also, you get major points for having top-notch taste in music," I say as we near the ski resort.

She blows on her fingernails then rubs them against her chest. "I do have most excellent taste."

"If you had said you liked Ed Sheeran or Coldplay, I'd have had second thoughts about our friendship."

Her eyes go wide and playful. "News flash. I do like Ed Sheeran."

I cringe as if she's said the worst thing in the world, because she kind of did. "I'm pretending you didn't just say that."

She shrugs. "I love Ed."

I shake my head adamantly. "Nope. You don't. You are a woman of the finest taste."

She shoots me a coy look. "I do have excellent taste."

And right now, I wish she'd act on that taste when it comes to the guy she's snowboarding with.

Except that can't happen.

* * *

When we hit the slopes, I swear we're a million miles away.

We spend the day zipping up the chair lift and then zooming down the hills, hopped up on adrenaline and by the possibility that snow brings.

After the final run, there's no way we can drive back to New York City.

As we head into the lodge, she says, "I guess we should stay the night."

"We should."

We reserve two rooms, and once we meet for dinner, it feels like everything's about to change.

INTERLUDE

Spencer

Things are about to change? I wonder what he could possibly mean by that.

That question will wait though. Because I've been dying to know about Savannah and Gavin's sleepover.

Call me crazy, but I don't think it's the kind that involves a sleeping bag. In fact, I wonder if they'll sleep at all.

22

GAVIN

I walk her up the steps, my hands on her hips. It takes a very long time to get to my apartment. The stairs creak and groan, especially because we stop every third or fourth one for a kiss. I kiss her behind her ear, and she shivers. I file that away, knowing I'll want to kiss her there again and find out if it elicits the same reaction.

She stops, turns, and plants a kiss on my lips. I nearly tumble backward because it's that powerful, and it goes to my head.

I steady myself. "I almost fell."

"You better not fall down the steps," she says.

"Get your ass up to my floor, then, and stop distracting me from . . . walking." I smack her ass.

"Far be it from me to distract you with my rear end."

"It's a highly distracting ass." We make it up a few

more steps when I tug on her jeans. "Just testing to see how quickly they come off."

"Why don't you find out once we're in your apartment?"

She's been here before. We've done the whole Netflix-and-chill thing. But we legit watched *Stranger Things*. Tonight, I'm pretty sure there's no Netflix ahead. Just chill.

Once we're inside my apartment, I reach for her, slide my hand around her waist, and bring her close.

We've kissed before, but this time I know it's not ending there. This time, I know we'll be making it to the other room. We'll find out what happens when friends turn into something more. It's scary and thrilling to know someone so well and for it to suddenly, or maybe not so suddenly at all, zoom to the next level.

I clasp my hands on her face and kiss her deeply, exploring her mouth, taking my time. As I do, I'm struck with a thought from out of left field.

I'll have a lifetime of kissing her.

Whoa.

I don't know why my brain leaped to that thought. I try to shake it off, because now isn't the time for contemplating futures and forevers.

But the thought stays in the back of my mind.

Or maybe it was there already, and now it's in the front of my head.

I can't let it go. Can't unsee it. Can't unfeel it.

Because this seems like the kind of kiss that won't end, that'll lead to more nights and days together.

This kiss feels like the start of our life together.

And I'd like it to include lots of kissing.

We find a rhythm quickly, a cocktail mix of soft and slow, then hard and fast, then deep and sweet. So damn sweet. I tug on the waistband of her jeans, breaking the kiss. "Okay, now I mean it. We need to get these off right now."

"You need to get *me* off right now," she says in a husky whisper.

I groan in appreciation, amazed that Savannah has this dirty piece to her. "I like learning this side of you."

She runs a hand up my chest, sending heat down my spine. "I like learning your sides too."

Once we're in the bedroom, we make quick work of our clothes. She's soft where she should be soft, and curvy where she should be curvy, and firm where I want her to be firm. But most of all, seeing her stripped bare does it for me. I go from rock hard to rock harder.

Judging from the way her eyes roam over my body, she likes what she sees too. She places her hands on my pecs, then trails them down my arms and back up to my face. "You're totally fucking hot."

"And totally fucking ready."

She slides her hand down my abs and grasps my erection. I close my eyes and shudder.

"That feels spectacular," she whispers.

"Couldn't agree more."

We make our way to the bed, and I find a condom, but I don't put it on right away.

We kiss more, touch more, explore each other. My hands map her body as they roam down her stomach, along her thighs, over the curve of her ass. She's just as frisky as I am, taking her own inventory, and we're both panting, groaning, and so damn aroused. I push her down on her back, grab her wrists, and thrust them over her head. "I need to get inside you now. I can't wait any longer."

She gives me a seductive, sexy smile. "So don't wait."

I roll on the condom and enter her.

Holy hell.

It takes me a moment to collect myself because this feels so damn good. And so right. I'm inside the woman who's been my best friend, who's been a fake date, who's been in the friend zone, and who's most definitely sliding all the way out of that zone tonight.

Because as I move with her, I'm keenly aware that it's not just fucking. I'm making love to her, and everything feels entirely different between us. When she says my name in that breathy gasp, I'm sure we're both feeling it, the same flash of possibility.

She loops her arms around my neck, pulls me close, and falls apart beneath me. I follow her there to the other side.

* * *

A little later, I run my hand through her hair and whisper in her ear. "I have a feeling we're going to be doing that for a long, long time," I say.

"Me too."

The next morning, after we say goodbye and I tell her I'll see her tonight, I call Eddie. "Dude, I have officially met the woman I'm going to marry, and I think you're going to love her."

"Dude, I already love the Sav-meister. She's awesome. Also, I knew it, and to celebrate how smart I am, I'm shopping for a new beer bong. Meet me at the diner and tell me all about it."

At lunch I make my announcement. "She's the one for me. It's that simple."

He slams a hand on the table and beams. "Knew it. Called it. Love it."

"Yeah, me too," I say.

* * *

The trouble is, once I propose a few months later and then ask Eddie to be my best man, he tells me he can't wait to share all my stories in front of our friends and family.

Gulp.

SAVANNAH

I can't stop staring at my ring. I show it off to Piper and Sloane one night over pool. Actually, I show it off every time I see them.

Well, they're both happily betrothed themselves, so it's all good.

"It's the size of a baseball," Sloane says.

"No, it's grown to dinosaur-egg size," Piper corrects.

I look at it yet again. "It's the world's most amazing ring. It gets bigger and better every time I look at it."

Sloane squeezes my shoulder. "That's because you *love* him more and more each day."

I go all soft inside. My heart is mushy, and it's wonderful. "I do. I really do."

Sloane arches a brow. Piper arches one of hers.

"So," Sloane begins, "this is where you admit it."

"Admit what?"

Piper laughs. "Oh, that's funny. Like you don't know."

"Don't know what?" I ask.

Sloane rolls her eyes. "It totally happened like a romance novel."

"Where everything turns into something," Piper puts in.

"Where fake dates lead to more," Sloane adds.

"And where true love wins the day."

What can I say? They were right. I square my shoulders. "You told me so."

They both clap and cheer.

And everything goes fabulously as we plan our wedding, until the night we're out to dinner with my parents, Gavin's parents, and Eddie.

After Eddie orders a beer, he chuckles.

"What's so funny?" my dad asks, amused and curious.

He lifts the glass. "Oh, I was just thinking about this time I bought a beer bong the size of a baseball bat. It was the best one ever. Got me wondering how quickly this brew would go down one. Hey! Idea! Should we do that at the wedding?"

My shoulders tighten. I meet Gavin's gaze. He nods at me, whispering an "I know."

We both know.

We're going to need a new best man.

Otherwise, everyone is going to know about the beer bong the size of a baseball bat and the plunger named Fred.

And really, those stories are best kept private.

After all, my crocheting aunt Ellen would likely faint, and we can't have that at our nuptials.

I run through the options with my fiancé, who's 100 percent onboard. Eddie is too. Wait, make that 110 percent on board. "Guys, I hate writing speeches. Plus, I'd rather dedicate all my focus on picking up bridesmaids," he says when we discuss the problem of Fred the plunger and the baseball bat–sized bong.

The next night over a plate of jalapeño nachos, Gavin and I debate replacements—other friends, and even colleagues. But everyone else feels wrong.

I turn to Piper. My good friend is a wedding planner after all. She *has* to know someone.

I meet her at a bookstore after work, where I find her flipping through a romance novel. She smiles then beckons me closer. "I have someone for you. I happen to be good friends with the city's premier best man for hire."

A few weeks later, Gavin and I meet her English friend at our favorite bar, where I'm instantly sold.

INTERLUDE

Spencer

All seems well, doesn't it? She's satisfied. He's satisfied. They swept past their issues. Even the issue of Eddie and the plunger and the beer bong.

That means we can chat about something else.

Let's talk about big gestures . . .

Say you're a gentleman of the world. Now say you reach that point in your wooing of a special lady where you're thinking it's time to go all in. To let her know. Maybe throw a parade.

Some women like parades.

Some women hate them.

What I'm saying is the gesture needs to matter to *her*.

The gesture may not be what you expect, but sometimes it's exactly what you need to do.

I nurse my drink at Gin Joint, reflecting on the helpful bartender's advice. She's busy catching up with another customer, an Englishman who seems to have come from a wedding, judging from the tux and bow tie.

"How did it go tonight? Were you charming and fabulously engaging, all while bestowing the necessary attention on the groom?" the bartender asks the man.

"Of course. I was thoroughly believable as I waxed poetic about what a fine chap he is and how I knew it'd last forever," he answers.

"There is no better best man for hire in all of Manhattan."

"None at all," he says.

I consider that job for a moment. An interesting career, to be sure. One I never knew existed.

"And when I told the story of the groom's big

gesture to win his bride's heart—the moment where he stood outside her window and professed his love— there was not a dry eye in the house."

That's interesting too.

Between this man's talk of big gestures and the bartender's remark about quitting my job, I start to formulate a plan.

By the time I finish my drink, I know what I need to do, thanks to the helpful bartender and her best man for hire. I don't know their names, but they both in their own way have given me exactly the advice I needed.

Yet a man must be a man of his word. As I leave the bar, I call Gigi and ask her to check the clause in my contract with Wu Media.

"You've fulfilled all your contractual obligations," my agent tells me. "But you do know you get a huge bonus if you exercise the option and re-up with the company?"

She tells me the figure, and it is tempting. But not as tempting as the woman I've fallen for.

"As long as I have done what I promised, then I must let the deal go."

I ask Gigi to tell the client, since that's the proper way to handle such matters.

After all, some things are bigger than work.

Bigger than brand campaigns.

She can't leave her company.

But I can.

25

VALERIE

I see red.

It billows out of my eyes and swirls around me.

My assistant has sent me an email from Enzo's agent about the termination of his contract, and I stare at it from my bed.

How could he simply up and quit? Is he going to leave the city and never come back? Will this be the last I see of him?

I dial Kingsley, and I tell her what he just did.

She fumes. "He better have a damn good reason."

"Right? How on earth could he just walk away from the contract without telling me first? We've become friends after all."

"You'd better march over to his place and see what it's all about."

"As if I'm doing anything else."

I say goodbye and hang up. I pull on a jacket, straighten my skirt, slide into my flats, and call my driver. Once outside on Fifth Avenue, I sweep into the car, slam the door in a dramatic fit of frustration, and give the address to Enzo's sublet. He's only been renting it for a few months—he hasn't even moved to New York. For all I know, he could be returning to Madrid.

Then it hits me.

He has all the reasons to leave. I haven't given him any to stay. Last time I saw him, I reminded him that we could only be friends.

Instantly, I change my mission. I need him to stay. I might be mad at him for walking away from his role as the face of my company when he could easily have re-upped with us for millions, but the idea of him leaving . . .

That ruins me.

A few minutes later, I arrive at the sleek skyscraper, thank my driver, and then head inside and tell the concierge I'm here to see Enzo De la Rosa.

The man gives me an impassive look. "Excellent. He's expecting you."

My brow furrows. "Expecting me?"

The man simply nods.

"How can he be expecting me?"

"He is."

I march to the elevator, press the button, and then head inside when the doors open. How on earth could he be expecting me?

But at least he hasn't left yet.

I ride up to the twelfth floor, step out of the elevator, head down the hall, and am about to bang on his door when he opens it, wearing a wicked grin.

"And what do you have to be so smiley-faced about? Because you're leaving me?" That came out a little tart. I guess I'm still annoyed.

He gestures to me. "Because you're here."

"I'm here because you didn't tell me first that you weren't continuing with Wu Media. I had to find out through my assistant that your agent said you're through. That's so upsetting, especially since I didn't get to tell you how I—"

He grabs me by the hand, tugs me inside, and kicks the door closed with his foot. He cups my cheeks. "No, what would be truly upsetting is if we never did this." He hauls me in for a kiss—an absolutely searing kiss that makes my body sing and my brain go haywire.

It's unexpected, but it's also completely inevitable. It's wondrous and hot, and it's wildly passionate too.

His lips explore mine as he bends me backward, taking over this kiss, letting me know that he's in charge.

He murmurs and moans, his tongue stroking inside my mouth, and all my systems go into overdrive.

My skin sizzles, my blood heats, and I'm hot everywhere. I'm enveloped in longing for this man as he kisses me with a fire that is not red-hot. It's white-hot.

I don't believe I've ever been kissed like this, but it is the only way a woman should ever be kissed.

He breaks away to say, "Don't you understand? I did it for you. I did it because I'm mad about you, Valerie. I'm crazy about you. Someone had to make the big gesture. It might as well be me."

I tremble. I'm filled with desire as well as something new. Emotions. Happiness. All at an intensity that says there is so much more to us than our newfangled friendship and our crazy chemistry. There's something brewing that could be real, that could be lasting. "You did it for me?"

He nods. "For us. You can't quit your company. But I can. So I did. I left so we no longer have anything between us."

My heart expands in my chest. "I came here to tell you not to leave. That we need to find a way to be together."

His grin grows impossibly wider. "This is the way. Because I did that all for us."

I run a hand through his hair, my tone softening even more. "You did that for us?"

"You mean so much more to me than a job. I want you more than work. And if that was our only barrier, it was my job as a man to knock it down."

I swoon.

I melt.

This man does everything to me. I set a hand on his chest, covering his heart. "You are the most incredible man I've ever met. And I want you to take me to bed."

He stares at me, his eyes smoldering, his expression full of desire. "In my bed, I will take you, and have you, and fuck you, and make love to you, and pleasure you all night long. I only have one rule."

"What's that?" I'm vibrating with lust.

He scoops me up in his arms and carries me, never breaking eye contact. "I'd like to be in charge of your pleasure."

"You can make all the rules."

In his bedroom, he strips me quickly, finds a tie, and binds my wrists to the bedposts.

He takes off his shirt, striding around in only a pair of shorts. "I want to marvel at how beautiful you look on my bed. And then I want to go down on you and taste you coming on my lips."

I shiver and grow even hotter when he crawls up the mattress, kissing me all over, kissing my neck, my breasts, then working his way down my body where he settles between my legs.

I'm going to go off like a rocket. He already has me so on edge, racing toward the finish line.

He presses his mouth against me, and I groan his name. Nothing has ever felt like this. It's like he's worshiping me. His moans are obscene and alluring at the same time, as he licks and kisses and sends me into overdrive.

I can't move my arms. Can't thread my hands through his hair. I want to, yet I love letting go as he consumes me. And I want to be consumed by him. Soon my legs are shaking and I'm flying, falling, breaking.

As I come down from the high, he crawls up me and whispers in my ear, "I want to have you every way possible. But right now, I need you on your hands and knees."

He unties me and flips me over, then he kisses his way down my back and thrusts two fingers inside me, as if he wants to make sure I'm ready. How could I be anything but ready after what he just did to me? He pushes down his boxers, grabs a condom, rolls it on, and slides inside me.

He groans, and it's the sexiest thing I've ever heard. It says he wants this as much as I want him.

And then he's fucking me like an animal, mounting me, gripping my waist.

He's taking me and having me, slapping my ass and pulling my hair and whispering filthy things in my ear about how much he's wanted to do this since he met me, about how he wants to do this every single night, about how I'm the sexiest woman he's ever met. About how he knows that what I need is to let go.

And I do let go as he rides me to the edge, then slows down, then does it again and again until I'm pretty much begging for him to let me come.

When he thrusts so far and so deep that I feel I might die if I don't come, I shudder, devastated by the intensity of my orgasm. Even more so when he joins me on this side of bliss.

But he's not all rough and tumble. He's not all dominant.

We make our way to the shower, where he runs soap all over my body then kisses me gently and tenderly.

"I want to make you feel good all the time, Valerie," he whispers. "Every day, every night. Always."

Like that, I'm ready again.

He takes me back to his bed.

This time, he makes love to me. He moves inside me, long and lingering, meeting my gaze.

"You're the only woman for me," he says.

It doesn't feel like a line from him. It feels like the truth. Especially when he takes me to Paris a few months later and tells me something even better.

26

ENZO

We reach the top of the Eiffel Tower.

Where else could I take my love but the most romantic city on earth? After all, there are so many art galleries here, each an opportunity to indulge in one of our favorite hobbies. She deserves everything, and I hope she will let me be the man to give that to her.

But tonight is for the icon of the city.

With all of Paris before us, I get down on one knee. "Valerie Wu, you are the most intoxicating woman I've ever known. And I want to make you happy for the rest of our lives. Would you do me the great honor of being my wife?"

Tears slide down her cheeks, and she clasps my face then tells me, "Yes."

I smile, filled with all the love and gratitude in the world. Then I'm filled with a new round of desire when she brings me in close for a kiss.

A kiss that turns hot instantly, as kisses with her do.

After we return to our hotel on the Left Bank and indulge in our other favorite hobby—yes, we enjoy the bedroom even more than art—I hum, a crease of worry on my brow as we discuss our wedding. "I think Sadie will be my bridesmaid. She's more than just an assistant these days," Valerie says.

"There's only one problem. I don't really know anybody in the United States. And you know everyone. I'm going to need a best man." And as soon as I voice that, a memory returns. A conversation I overheard.

I prop my head in my hand. "Wait. I have an idea. Have you ever heard of a best man for hire?"

"I have. And that sounds like a perfect solution. Let me have Sadie do some googling and find the best one for us," she says with a twinkle in her eye.

"You don't mind looking into it?"

She runs a hand down my chest. "Darling, it would be my pleasure."

I growl and kiss her once more.

But she breaks the kiss. "There's only one thing I want from you."

"Name it."

"Remember when you go on your next photo shoot, indulge me by sending a selfie. I do love seeing your handsome face when you're out of town."

I drop a kiss to her lips. How did I get so lucky? She's perfect for me in every single way.

When I'm in Milan the next week, I pose for her and send her a shot.

She responds with more emojis than I've ever seen. Her delight feeds my desire to make her happy.

Then she tells me she's booked the best man for hire.

Enzo: You are a goddess.

I'm a lucky man. I have a solid job. I've risen from less-than-ideal circumstances. And now I have this fantastic woman. The only thing left to do is to make it all official when we walk down the aisle.

I send her one more selfie, this one a little naughtier.

Valerie: You better get home soon because I have some serious plans for you.

Enzo: No, my love. I have incredible plans for you. Every single night I see you.

INTERLUDE

Spencer

And it looks like our fabulously wealthy CEO worked out her issues with her . . . oh, come on. He's not a boy toy. He's a mogul too. A superstar model, and he scored the woman he digs.

Their flirtation turned into something much more. From selfies to art to pizza to true love. They found their way, and they're moving into the next chapter.

They only have one more hurdle to cross, but it seems they already found their solution in a certain best man for hire.

Hmm. I wonder who that might be.

I have my suspicions. I suspect, too, that all these stories are about to collide. But there's one more facet to this gem of instant attraction.

Jason and Truly spent their afternoon in the land

of soft mounds of snow and hard, polished boards to plow through them.

And then they said they were just going to dinner.

Sure, sometimes dinner is just dinner.

But sometimes it's the start of something else, and the question is whether the flame will catch tonight or if it's going to be a long, slow burn.

27

JASON

It's just dinner.

Steak and salad.

Risotto and peas.

It's just what we do to feed ourselves, because we're hungry after a day on the slopes.

That's all. It shouldn't feel like a dinner date. It *doesn't* feel like a dinner date. Or so I tell myself as I button my long-sleeved shirt then tuck it into my jeans.

We have separate rooms, and I'm simply going down to meet a friend for dinner at the lodge. The cozy mountain lodge. The romantic, cozy mountain lodge with fireplaces everywhere.

Fucking hell.

As I walk downstairs from my second-floor room, I imagine I have blinders on, ignoring all these fireplaces. Besides, what's so romantic about fireplaces anyway? They're sooty and ashy, and they require a lot of upkeep. They make a place so damn hot that you're sweating, and you have to take off your clothes.

Oh.

Yeah.

That.

It would be ridiculously fucking sexy if Truly took off her clothes because she was too hot.

I better not think about that at all. That's precisely why I can't go there. She's just one of the guys.

I repeat this mantra over and over.

Just one of the guys, just one of the guys, just one of the guys.

But when she heads down the stairs wearing jeans, boots, and a bulky fisherman's sweater, I gesture to the offending attire. "Would you like me to burn that sweater before or after dinner?"

With wide eyes, she plucks at the material. "What's wrong with my sweater?"

I tap my chin. "Hmm, where to start? It's bulky, for one."

She waves toward the windows, which are edged with frost. "It's cold outside."

"It's shapeless."

She shrugs. "So? Do you want me to show you my shape?"

Don't answer that.

"It's . . . well. Actually . . ." I slow my mouth down, because the sweater is perfect. It's one of the least sexy things I've ever seen. "You're just one of the guys in that sweater."

She gives me a strange, not-quite smile. "Gee, that's what I've always wanted to be." But then it turns to a full grin. "Actually, it's good if you think of me as just one of the guys. We can keep focusing on the friendship."

Instead of on my texts about kissing her.

We head into the restaurant, and the hostess seats us then hands us the menus. Candles flicker, so I continue my efforts to dismiss all notions of romance. "Why are candles romantic? They're just fire hazards, if you think about it."

See? I'm all about friendship.

She pats my arm. "Don't worry, Jason. I have on the ugly sweater, and we have fire hazards. There's not a chance this could be construed as romantic. But while we're discussing clothes that should be burned, can we talk about that gray T-shirt of yours? The one with the holes in it?"

I shoot her an inquisitive look. "I don't own a holey shirt."

Her blue eyes twinkle. "Oh, but you do."

I shake my head. "No, I don't."

She nods again. "You do. You wore it to spin class."

"I did?"

Before she can respond, the waiter arrives and asks for our order. I opt for chicken, and she chooses pasta. And when he walks away, I arch a brow. "Where were the alleged holes in this T-shirt?"

She pats my biceps. "Right here."

I lift a brow. "You were checking out my biceps.

Admit it. You love my arms," I say, then curse myself. That's not guy-talk.

She rolls her eyes. "I was not."

I flex my muscles, giving myself a break for a moment. "See? Pretty damn good, aren't they?"

She reaches out her hand and squeezes. "Yes, your arms are fabulous. Besides, why are you so upset about your holey shirt? You attacked my bulky sweater. I'll attack your shirt."

"Fair play," I say, leaning back in the chair, thoroughly enjoying our banter. I simply won't make any more flirty remarks, nor any kissing ones. No way. No how. I've got this.

We chat some more, about clothes that ought to be burned and food we don't think should exist and mountains we want to snowboard on, and it's friendly, with *only* a little bit of flirtation thrown in. Because I can't help myself.

And that seems to be par for the course with us.

Just because I sent those texts doesn't mean I'll backslide again.

Even though we're at this *supposedly* romantic lodge.

But I'm not worried. I haven't even had anything to drink, and I keep it that way all through dinner.

* * *

When the meal ends, I pay the bill, and Truly waves

her hand in front of her face, fanning herself. "It's soooo hot. These fireplaces are pretty damn strong."

Uh-oh.

She reaches down and tugs off her sweater. I close my eyes for a second, hoping she's not wearing something ridiculously sexy like a camisole. Do women even wear camisoles under bulky fisherman sweaters? I don't know. If they don't, maybe they should. Pretty women should just wear camisoles all the time.

I open my eyes as she tugs her sweater over her head.

My jaw falls open. She's wearing . . . my holey gray T-shirt. I point that out, surprised. "You have on my T-shirt."

She looks down at the material. "Oh, this old thing? I was just going to burn it later."

I narrow my eyes. "You'll do no such thing. That's a very special T-shirt."

"Why is it such a special T-shirt? It's full of holes."

"Well, why are you wearing it, then?"

"Because you left it at my house after we did the spin class."

"And you held on to it. Admit it, you haven't even washed it."

"Actually, I did wash it before this trip, and I brought it here to give back to you. And I thought it would be kind of funny to wear to dinner. But I was cold, so I put on the sweater. And now that you've said you hate my sweater, maybe I should just keep your shirt."

"Well, it does look fucking foxy on you," I say, and yep, there's some quicksand.

"You think it looks foxy on me?" she asks as we exit the restaurant and head for the stairs.

I eye her in her jeans, her boots, and my T-shirt, which only has one little hole in the arm. "Yeah," I say, tracing the hole, touching a sliver of her skin. Seems my shoe is grazing that slope. "There's just something incredibly sexy when a woman wears a man's clothes."

She looks at me. "Why is that?"

And here I go, one foot leaving solid ground. "I think it's something about marking a woman. I guess it makes it feel like . . ." I stop myself. Am I really going to go here? Am I really going to say this?

Evidently I'm sliding all the way. "It makes me feel like you're mine. It makes it look like you tugged that on after I fucked you."

Apparently I don't need champagne to loosen my lips.

She stops at the top of the steps. "So does this T-shirt make something a foregone conclusion, then?"

I stare at her, at this woman I've been wildly attracted to since I met her, at this woman who's become my great friend and who is my best friend's sister.

But in this moment, she's none of those things. She's the woman I want to mark. She's the woman I want to make mine. She's the woman who I want to be wearing my clothes right after I fuck her.

I reach for the hem of the shirt, tug her close, and

say, "Yeah, I hope it does." She's inches from me, and this is the moment of truth. The moment *before*. We stare at each other, hovering on that edge where we can still step back and return to being friends.

She's just one of the guys, she's just one of the guys, she's just one of the guys.

But she's not one of the guys. She's the woman I desperately want.

One more tug, and then she steps forward into my arms and seals her lips to mine.

It's instant—I'm hotter than the fireplace. Flames flicker across my skin, blazing through my body. I slide a hand into her hair, bring her even closer, and slam my mouth to hers, kissing her fiercely, kissing her ferociously. I kiss her like it's the thing I've wanted to do for years, because it is.

We kiss deep and hard, without any pretense, without any build. We're already there. We didn't start at zero, but we went straight to sixty, and now we're speeding along this highway of kissing—mouths ravenous, tongues exploring, hands everywhere.

Her fingers slide along my arms, along my neck, into my hair, tugging and pulling. I'm lit up everywhere, crackling and sizzling with desire for her. I break the kiss and point in the general direction of the hallway. "Room. Now."

Before I know it, we're inside her room, and I push her up against the door and strip off the T-shirt then tug down her jeans and underwear. Her hands move quickly, unbuttoning my shirt and pushing down my jeans too. I kiss her neck, inhaling her delicious, luscious scent.

I thread a hand through her hair, look her in the eyes, and say, "You need to know I've wanted you since the first night I met you."

She nods savagely, panting. "God, I'm so incredibly attracted to you, it's ridiculous."

I slam my pelvis against her, letting her feel what she does to me. "It's insane."

She pushes down my briefs, grabs my ass, and pulls me closer. "Do you have a condom? Because if you do, it would be great if you could get it on and then get inside me right now."

That's really all she needs to say.

The hotel provides condoms, but I have one too. Not because I expected to have sex with her. But because a man should always be prepared. In a few seconds, I rip it open, roll it on, and then I position myself between her legs, rubbing the head against her slippery sweetness, savoring our heat. "Oh, you really do want to be fucked tonight."

She nods. "I really want *you* to fuck me."

I push inside her, heat shooting all over my body as I fill her. Rocking, stroking, and thrusting—all I think about is her and the sheer intensity of this moment. We're like a wire stretched to its limit, and all the tension of the last few years snaps as we come together at last. She pants, and I groan. Our bodies collide, moving together in a powerful, intoxicating rhythm.

She grabs at my hair, telling me, "Harder, faster, there, right there, now."

I do as instructed, giving the woman what she wants until she's shouting my name and coming hard.

We don't stop there. I bring her to the couch and bend her over it. She offers up her body so deliciously, her ass in the air, lovely and succulent, and I want to bite it and smack it and kiss it. I bend down and nibble on her rear, then get right back inside her.

She claws at the cushions and rocks back against me.

"Use your fingers too," she tells me.

I groan in pleasure. "There's nothing I love more than when a woman knows exactly what she wants."

"I know exactly what I want. I want you to make me come again."

This is too much. This is so fucking good. This is the way it should be. Open, honest, fierce. *Passionate.*

I bring a hand between her legs and touch her where she wants me most until she goes flying again and I follow her there.

We pant and moan, and it takes ages to come down.

But we do, and I turn on the fireplace, bring her over to the couch, and pull her close.

This time we're a little slower, a little more deliberate, but it's still just as delicious. And the next best part? We don't dissect it. We don't freak out. She doesn't say anything like *Oh, holy shit, we shouldn't have done that.* Instead she says, "I think that was a long time in the making."

"Years, I'd say."

Later, we move to the shower and we kiss more there, exploring each other. She moans and purrs like a cat. "Tonight exists in another world, doesn't it?" she asks softly.

"Yeah, it does. Let's keep enjoying it, okay?"

Once we're out of the shower, I bring her to the bed. She is spectacular in all of her naked glory and I need to have her again. I kiss her all over. Her neck, her throat, her breasts, her belly. And then I spread her legs open, and I taste her delicious sweetness, drinking her pleasure on my tongue.

She's hot and wet and needy. She arches up against me, saying my name, asking for more, moaning and groaning and telling me not to stop.

As if I would.

I send her over the edge again, and then she sits up, straddles me, and grabs another condom. Just like that, she rides me hard, and it's a gorgeous sight.

This is one of those nights when you don't want to sleep.

When you spend the entire night fucking, and it's exactly what an entire night of fucking should be.

It is the best night ever.

The only problem is the morning comes.

28

TRULY

I squint.

The sun blinds me.

It streams through the window.

Shining a light on last night.

On tangled sheets. Condom wrappers. Clothes strewn on the floor.

Awareness slams into me.

"Malone would kill us," I say, worry gripping my chest.

"Yeah, he would," Jason seconds.

Only, that's not entirely true. I don't think my brother would hate us. I don't even know how upset he would be.

But *I'm* upset. Because I've done something I swore I'd never do. I've broken a promise to myself and a promise I made to others. I can't let something like that happen again, no matter how much I want Jason. "Can we agree that last night was amazing?"

"It was incredible."

"But it can't happen again," I say.

He sits, nodding reluctantly. "I agree. It can't happen again."

I breathe a sigh of relief. "Good."

"Did you think I would feel otherwise?"

"No, I'm glad you feel the same. We have to go back to being just friends, Jason."

"Yeah. This was just a lapse . . . We were away for the day. We weren't in New York. It was the snow—blame it on the snow."

I laugh. "We can definitely blame it on the snow. And those fireplaces."

* * *

We drive back to Manhattan, and it's as if the night rewinds like a roll of film.

We reenact the drive up, singing along to the Rolling Stones and the Beatles and remaking the fabric of our friendship.

By the time we arrive in New York City, last night is just a memory.

"I think we did it. We're the textbook case for friends getting caught up in the moment and then returning to the friend zone," I say.

He offers a hand to high-five. "We are definitely back in the friend zone." And that's where we stay for the next six months, until the night he walks into my bar with a proposition.

EPILOGUE

Spencer

That's the story of how three different couples found their happily ever afters, and how instant attraction seems to have worked out for all of them.

Enzo and Valerie will be walking down the aisle any day now. Same for Gavin and Savannah. And, well, Jason and Truly . . . they can zip right back into the friend zone, no problem. Right?

You'll have to stay tuned. Because that proposition Truly mentioned? It involves her attending a couple weddings with the guy who's "just a friend."

That should work out fine . . . as long as there's no unfinished business between them, which I expect there is. Enough unfinished business for another chapter in the book of dirty fairy tales.

In fact, I bet there's a nice, long, delicious, twisty, sexy modern romance there.

How it turns out though . . . I won't take bets on that. You'll have to turn the page and find out what happens when these three couples meet.

Until then, have sweet, dirty dreams.

THE END. FOR NOW.

JASON AND TRULY'S STORY CONTINUES IN INSTANT GRATIFICATION, available everywhere.

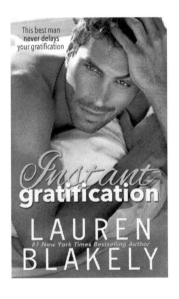

Want to be the first to learn of sales, new releases, preorders and special freebies? Sign up for my VIP mailing list here!

ALSO BY LAUREN BLAKELY

FULL PACKAGE, the #1 New York Times Bestselling romantic comedy!

BIG ROCK, the hit New York Times Bestselling standalone romantic comedy!

MISTER O, also a New York Times Bestselling standalone romantic comedy!

WELL HUNG, a New York Times Bestselling standalone romantic comedy!

JOY RIDE, a USA Today Bestselling standalone romantic comedy!

HARD WOOD, a USA Today Bestselling standalone romantic comedy!

THE SEXY ONE, a New York Times Bestselling bestselling standalone romance!

THE HOT ONE, a USA Today Bestselling bestselling standalone romance!

THE KNOCKED UP PLAN, a multi-week USA Today and Amazon Charts Bestselling bestselling standalone romance!

MOST VALUABLE PLAYBOY, a sexy multi-week USA

Today Bestselling sports romance! And its companion sports romance, MOST LIKELY TO SCORE!

THE V CARD, a USA Today Bestselling sinfully sexy romantic comedy!

WANDERLUST, a USA Today Bestselling contemporary romance!

COME AS YOU ARE, a Wall Street Journal and multi-week USA Today Bestselling contemporary romance!

PART-TIME LOVER, a multi-week USA Today Bestselling contemporary romance!

UNBREAK MY HEART, an emotional second chance USA Today Bestselling contemporary romance!

BEST LAID PLANS, a sexy friends-to-lovers USA Today Bestselling romance!

The Heartbreakers! The USA Today and WSJ Bestselling rock star series of standalone!

The New York Times and USA Today
Bestselling Seductive Nights series including
Night After Night, *After This Night*,
and *One More Night*

And the two standalone
romance novels in the Joy Delivered Duet, *Nights With Him*

and Forbidden Nights, both New York Times and USA Today Bestsellers!

Sweet Sinful Nights, Sinful Desire, Sinful Longing and Sinful Love, the complete New York Times Bestselling high-heat romantic suspense series that spins off from Seductive Nights!

Playing With Her Heart, a

USA Today bestseller, and a sexy Seductive Nights spin-off standalone! (Davis and Jill's romance)

21 Stolen Kisses, the USA Today Bestselling forbidden new adult romance!

Caught Up In Us, a New York Times and

USA Today Bestseller! (Kat and Bryan's romance!)

Pretending He's Mine, a Barnes & Noble and

iBooks Bestseller! (Reeve & Sutton's romance)

My USA Today bestselling

No Regrets series that includes

The Thrill of It

(Meet Harley and Trey)

and its sequel

Every Second With You

My New York Times and USA Today

Bestselling Fighting Fire series that includes

Burn For Me

(Smith and Jamie's romance!)

Melt for Him

(Megan and Becker's romance!)

and *Consumed by You*

(Travis and Cara's romance!)

The Sapphire Affair series...

The Sapphire Affair

The Sapphire Heist

Out of Bounds

A New York Times Bestselling sexy sports romance

The Only One

A second chance love story!

Stud Finder

A sexy, flirty romance!

CONTACT

I love hearing from readers! You can find me on Twitter at LaurenBlakely3, Instagram at LaurenBlakelyBooks, Facebook at LaurenBlakelyBooks, or online at LaurenBlakely.com. You can also email me at laurenblakelybooks@gmail.com

30210002R00104

Printed in Great
Britain
by Amazon